A CONTINUATION TRILOGY

ILA'S DIAMONDS IV

"THE HOUSE THAT JACK BUILT"

DONNA M. GRAY-BANKS

www.LeesPress.net

A Premiere Self-Publishing Services Company

ISBN-13:

Paperback

ILA'S DIAMONDS IV

"THE HOUSE THAT JACK BUILT"

Acknowledgments

To my brother Gilbert W. Gray and sister Christine Hogan (Westinghouse Forever)

To my son, Gregory Taylor Banks, you are my major accomplishment.

My mother, Lorraine; my father, Jackson W. Gray, Sr.,

My nephew, Gary L. Hogan and my baby brother Jackson W. Gray, Jr., who have all transitioned.

My niece, Tomika Freeman - Bravery unsurpassed

My GFFL - Friendship enough said.

To Robert Banks - It was significant.

To Alan J. Price - Thank you for the inspiration.

Dr. Seuss - Thank you.

To The Creator - God's Grace Is Sufficient

"When the lights go out and the cell phone towers go down, all you have left is a flashlight and a good book?" **—Ila**

Eugenia wanted to look her best for Ila. She was looking for her eyeshadow but found her curling iron. She planned to curl her hair anyway. She needed to put gel in it so the style would last all night. She found everything she needed and went to work. She was incredibly pleased at the result, even though it took about an hour. She was so jealous of Stephen. All he did was take a shower. He was now watching TV, still not dressed. She was sure he had a nice suit to put on, but it would only take him twenty minutes to do that. She came out of the bathroom and walked to the living room. He looked at her and laughed.

"You look fabulous! I have never seen you wear that much makeup. If I had a camera, I'd take a picture." Eugenia picked up a pillow and hit him with it.

Suddenly Stephen said, "Be quiet!"

There was a breaking news story on TV—"two men had been found in the Marriott Hotel in gangland-style killing: "The men were found after several complaints from other hotel guests about a horrible smell coming from the room. The maintenance men entered the room and found the two men in the bathroom. More details will be given as they become available." Stephen looked at Eugenia and said, "Believe me, when the police look at their credentials and the appropriate authorities are called, this will go in the back pages of the Washington Post." They both laughed and went on to get ready for the wedding. They were both ready around 4:30 pm, and Stephen put all of their stuff in the car. He wore a silver sharkskin suit, a black shirt, a silver tie, and Stacy Adams black-and-white shoes. He looked so handsome. He refused to go to the wedding without his holster and gun, and he wore his .22 on his ankle. Eugenia thought that was overkill but considering the bodies that had just been found, she understood that he could be a little paranoid. Eugenia could not leave the house without a gun either. She decided to strap her .22 to her ankle. The guns were loaded but not locked because they did not have locks. When these guns were cocked, you were ready to let go on something or someone. Eugenia did not want to mess up her pedicure even though the nail polish was dry. She put on her hold-it-in underwear and a good bra. Then she put on her blue jeans and a button-down shirt, so she didn't have to take anything over her head. She put on her leather jacket with a scarf, grabbed her garment bag, and was ready to go. Stephen grabbed his leather coat, took off his suit jacket and hung it on a hanger. He would hang up his suit jacket in the car. They were ready to go. They would just sit in the car and wait for Ila. They headed toward the door, made sure the apartment was secure, and headed out. It had gotten colder because the sun had gone down, and it was getting dark. Ila was blessed; it had not snowed. It was just chilly, and there was a full moon, which would make for beautiful pictures after the wedding, if they could stand to be in the cold for a few minutes. They walked down the stairs and put everything in the trunk. Stephen hung his coat in the backseat. Eugenia had gotten into the passenger side, which he thought was interesting. She was really nesting; now she wanted to be driven around. He laughed to himself. It was not long before they saw Ila coming down the steps. She looked so happy. She walked to the car and motioned for Eugenia to roll the window down. She stuck her head in the car and said, "I have to make two trips." She put her first load in the car and hurried back upstairs to get her second load. She did not want to leave the silver Nike's behind. They would be such a great gift after the wedding, along with the bracelets, which she planned to give to Paula and Eugenia before they walked down the aisle. She grabbed the bags and turned right around and went back out the door. She remembered to turn on the outside light by the back door, then she locked the door and headed to the car. Stephen and Eugenia were laughing—probably laughing at her. She put the rest of her bags into the backseat. She had so much stuff she had to go on the other side and sit behind Eugenia. They were still laughing when Ila got into the car. Ila said, "You guys laughing at me?" They both said, "Yes!" Stephen said, "It looks like you're taking the entire apartment to the wedding." Ila had to laugh with them. It was a lot of stuff. Stephen turned over the engine and pulled out of the parking space.

They were all very quiet. There was such a feeling of finality among those in the car. Stephen and Eugenia knew they would never have to worry about Hunter and Maurice again. Ila was thinking that, once they all got reassigned, it may be years before they would see each other again. It made her a little sad. It did not take them long to get to the back gate at the university, which was a blessing because the chapel was not far from there. Ila got really excited when she saw all the activity—a food truck, employees dressed in all black, students hanging around waiting for the chapel doors to open. She hoped they would open the doors soon. It was cold out in the parking area. Stephen parked as close to the door as he could so he could help Ila and Eugenia get all their things out of the car. When Ila got out of the car, she could hear one of the students' yell, "Ms. Montgomery, tell them to please open the door." Ila yelled back, "I'll see what I can do." They all yelled, "Thank you!" Ila picked up her two bags, Stephen grabbed both the garment bags, and Eugenia picked up Ila's extra bag and the tennis shoes. She looked in the bag and then looked at Ila. Ila said, "You were not supposed to see them, but since you have, I know you'll really enjoy them." They both laughed. They walked up to the huge wooden doors. There was a security officer at the door. He said, "Hello, Ms. Montgomery. Congratulations." Ila said, "Thank you very much. Is there any way we can let the students in from the cold?" He said, "The chef didn't want the students to start eating the food before the ceremony began. You know how students are." Ila said, "Yes, but it is really cold out here, and they are my invited guests. Why don't you come in and stand in the hallway where the food is going to be served and direct them to the chapel. There are bathrooms right before the chapel, so there won't be any reason for them to go any further." He thought about that for a second and said, "Okay. You go get settled in the bridal room, and I'll start letting them in." Ila smiled and said, "Thank you so much. It means so much to me." With that, Stephen handed him a hundred-dollar bill and said, "Happy New Year! Thank you for working today. You could have been home with your family, but you chose to help Ms. Montgomery on her wedding day. Thanks so much." Ila and Eugenia looked at each other. Wow, what a great thing to do. Stephen was accumulating more brownie points. All Eugenia and Ila could do was laugh. Between the three of them they only had to make one trip with all the items Ila and Eugenia had brought with them. They entered the chapel, which had been decorated in white carnations. There was a bouquet attached to every pew. And out of nowhere the photographer appeared taking pictures. He introduced himself as "Mr. Snap." They all laughed and said it was nice to meet him. "I just want to get some before pictures if you don't' mind. Eugenia and Ila started posing, making faces, and acting really crazy. Just then they heard, "Don't start without me!" And in ran Paula. Her hair was wrapped, and she was wearing tennis shoes with the toes cut out. They were laughing so hard; they didn't realize that Stephen had taken all the items into the bridal room and had disappeared. Ila, Paula, and Eugenia posed for several more pictures and stopped when the students started filing into the chapel. Ila looked down the aisle and noticed that the first three rows on both sides were roped off with white rope. She wondered why they had done that. Then it dawned on her—those seats were saved for the family of the bride and groom. She had not told anyone that neither she nor Brock had family members coming. In any event, it all looked beautiful. The lights had been dimmed except for the light on the altar. It was a sight that Ila would never forget. The ladies turned and went into the bridal room. As they were chatting and touching up their makeup and hair, a tear slowly fell down Paula's face. She said, "Drew said to tell you that he's here, congratulations, and he loves you." Ila looked at Paula and said, "If Drew is here, tell him to get out the room and stop looking at naked women!" They all laughed. Ila didn't want to get sentimental, but she knew that Paula could feel Drew at every step because they had been inseparable during their time together. It was about 6:15 when the photographer knocked on the door. "Come in," Ila said. Mr. Snap said he had just taken pictures of the groom and his best man and was now ready to snap pictures of the bride and her party. The ladies were ready. He took individual pictures and then he took pictures of them together. There was a second knock at the door. It was a young lady dressed in black who brought in their bouquets. They were stunning. The frilly petals of Ila's white carnations had been trimmed in silver, and a silver ribbon ran through the bouquet. Ila almost lost it but held it together. Paula held her hand tight. And that reminded Ila of the bracelets and tennis shoes. She pulled the bracelets out of one of the bags and called her friends over. "This is just a small token of our appreciation because you are sharing this magnificent day with us. We are very grateful," Ila said. With that, she handed them their boxes. Paula and Eugenia opened their gifts at the same time and gasped. The bracelets were beautiful. They put the bracelets on each other and thanked Ila like crazy. Ila handed them the shoe boxes. "I just wanted you to know that I thought you guys would probably kick off these beautiful silver boots immediately after the wedding, so we got you silver tennis shoes to wear after the ceremony." Ila laughed. The ladies were very grateful because those boots were made for looking at, not walking in. They laughed and hugged each other. All the while the photographer was taking pictures.

There was another knock at the door, and the same lady in black said, "We are ready. It's six thirty." Ila looked at Paula and Eugenia and said, "Show time!" The lady opened the door. A melodic voice starting to sing "Ava Maria" accompanied by the rich tones of the organ. Eugenia was first to head down the aisle. She could see Brock and Morris at the altar. She also saw Stephen standing in the middle pew at the end of the row, looking handsome and smiling at her. She got misty eyed. Would this ever happen for her? Once Eugenia got to the white rope, she made a left and stood at the altar. Then the lady motioned for Paula to start her descent down the long, beautiful aisle. Ila stood in the doorway to the bridal room and was amazed at how many students had showed up. She was so excited; her heart was beating fast, and her mouth had gone dry. Just then the lady in black handed her a small water glass with a straw. She smiled at Ila. Ila took several sips and was very grateful for the water. This lady had done this a thousand times before. Once Paula was at the rope and turning left, Ila came out of the foyer and stood for a minute, her eyes glued to Brock.

Brock and Morris had to take naps because they had shared one too many shots. They did not wake up until there was a persistent knock at the door. Brock jumped up, grabbed his gun, stood alongside the door, and shouted. "Who is it?" The person on the other side said, "Laundry." Brock laughed to himself and opened the door slowly. Morris had jumped up and grabbed his wallet to give the young lady a tip. He took the tuxedos from her and handed her a ten-dollar bill while Brock stayed behind the door, gun still in his hand. The young lady left, and they both laughed. "Shades of old times," Morris said. Morris took his tuxedo to one room and Brock's to another. It was 4:15 p.m.; they had to hurry. They both jumped in the shower and got dressed. The tuxedos fit them perfectly. Brock could not believe how good they looked. They were so used to seeing each other in jeans, leather coats, and tennis shoes or boots. Brock's hair had grown in just right, and Morris was wearing a well-shaped afro. He picked it for a second and said to his reflection in the mirror, "Perfection." They laughed. Brock had put Morris's bracelet and the rings on the table. He picked up the box that held the bracelet and said, "Man, this is just a token to let you know how happy I am that you could join us. Thanks for being my brother, friend, and confidant for almost twenty years. That is rare, and I want you to know I don't take it lightly." They hugged, and Brock handed him the box. Morris pulled out the bracelet and put it on his wrist. There was nothing left to say except, "Let's ride." They laughed. Brock put on his holster and gun. He slipped his leather jacket on, keeping his tuxedo jacket on its hanger. Morris, on the other hand, did not want to wear a holster. He decided to carry his Glock in his jacket pocket for now. He would put it behind his back in his belt during the ceremony so it would not look like a bulge in his jacket. Morris was a little vain. He had to laugh to himself about that. They stood at the table and took another shot before they headed for the door. They rode down the elevator and laughed about old times. They had parked in the garage, so they got off on that floor. Morris said, "Man, you know I have to rush back to the room after dinner, get my things, and catch the redeye back to California." Brock nodded. "Man, I wish you could stay, but for now we're going to enjoy this evening. We'll get you to the transport on time." They walked to the car and could not help but look in the car windows to look at themselves. It was clear they had it going on. It was 6:10 p.m. It would take them ten minutes to get to the university. After hanging their coats up in the back, they both jumped into the car. The ride to the university was smooth, but Brock was surprised as he drove to the back gate at how many people were there—catering trucks, students, catering workers, security personnel. Everyone was scurrying around. Brock showed his credentials at the gate, and the security guard said, "Congratulations! You're a lucky man." Brock said, "Thank you!" He shook his head and said to Morris, "That Ila has a way with the men. I'm going to have to put her in a tower like Rapunzel." Morris did not say a word, but to himself, he said, "Fat chance that's going to happen." He laughed out loud. Brock said, "What's so funny?" Morris said, "I had a visual of that Rapunzel thing … that was funny." They both laughed. They parked as close to the door as they could; the parking lot was full. They jumped out of the car, and the security guard motioned for them to go on the other side of the building to the other entrance. Brock and Morris hurried to the other door. Inside stood a woman in black. The ceiling of the foyer was a glass dome. Brock looked up and looked at the stars. For a minute he thought he saw a shooting star. He believed that was good luck. The lady had the flowers for their lapels in boxes. She led them to a little room behind the altar. At 6:30 p.m. they would walk out to the altar and wait for Paula and Eugenia, and then the bride. The lady said she would be back in five minutes. That gave them time to get into their tux jackets, pin on their boutonnieres, secure their guns, check themselves in the mirror, and hug again. It seemed that the lady left and came right back. She said, "Gentleman, it is time." Brock and Morris walked through the door and stood at the altar. Out of nowhere, a beautiful black woman dressed in all white started singing "Ava Maria." The pipe organ was loud. Everyone could feel the keys pumping the music out into the chapel. The lady in black stood in the middle of the aisle and motioned for everyone to stand up. That was the moment Brock saw Eugenia head down the aisle. She looked gorgeous—beautiful and deadly. His heart was pounding so hard he thought everyone could hear it. Then he felt the rub on his back from Morris, and his heart slowed down. Eugenia came to the end of the aisle and made a left to the altar just as Paula made her way down the aisle looking ghetto fabulous. She was Ila's best friend. She had tears in her eyes. He could not look at her because he would also tear up. Paula stood to the left of the altar next to Eugenia. Then, the music stopped, and the organist played a snippet of Wagner's traditional "Bridal Chorus," after which she and the vocalist switched back to "Ava Maria." It was fabulous, so well done. Brock finally looked up and locked eyes with Ila. She was so beautiful, and he knew at that moment that he had done the right thing. He felt Morris' tension change. He looked back and Morris smiled.

Ila was midway down the aisle when she looked at the man

behind Brock. Her knees turned to Jell-O. Oh, my God! It's Rodney! She stood still for a moment. They looked at each other, and Rodney shook his head. As Ila regained her composure, Stephen jumped up to help her down the aisle. He grabbed her by the arm and said, "It would be my pleasure to give you away." Ila looked at him and said, "Thank you so much." She locked eyes on Brock, and a tear rolled down her face. How could this shit happen? Rodney noticed that Stephen's pant legs were uneven—the leg on the right was almost dragging his ankle as if he had something heavy in his right-hand pocket. Rodney was thinking, who is this motherfucker? He waited until they got to the end of the aisle. Then he reached behind his back, grabbed his gun, and held it down next to his right leg. He could easily put it back behind his back after they said, "I do" and everyone was looking at them. The Pastor entered from a side door and stood ready to receive the bride and groom. The singer finished the last stanza of "Ava Maria," and the pipe organ stopped. The non-denominational Pastor was obviously not prepared to ask the traditional question: "Who gives this bride away?" He had been told that Ila would walk down the aisle alone. Brock turned to look at the Pastor, and so did Ila. Stephen still had her hand. The Pastor began: "Doubly blessed is the couple who comes to the marriage altar with the approval and blessing of family members, friends, and students. Who has the honor of presenting this woman to this man for the honor of marriage?"

All the students called out, "We do!" Stephen placed Ila's hand in Brock's hand. At the same time, Stephen took his .22 out of his pocket and shot Brock in the stomach two times.

"This is for the chief, motherfucker!" he said. Someone screamed, "Gun!" Eugenia hit the floor and pulled her gun out of her ankle holster. Paula was motionless as was the Pastor. The students began to run out of the chapel as security personnel ran down the aisle. Rodney aimed his Glock and shot Stephen in the middle of his head. Stephen dropped to the floor. Brock had let go of Ila's hand. He was falling to the floor. Blood was dripping off her face onto her dress. One of the security guards reached the altar. Rodney dropped his gun because the security guard did not know who the shooter was. As paramedics and police officers started running into the chapel, Ila collapsed.

Rodney had no time to waste. He looked around for an exit. There was so much going on, he felt he could slip away. Out of nowhere came Mr. Snap, who no longer had a camera but had a Glock. He grabbed Rodney by the elbow and walked him quickly behind the altar into a back office. He looked at Mr. Snap and said, "What Rivers Run North," Mr. Snap said, "St. Johns and the Nile." He grabbed Rodney by the elbow again and hurried him out the back door. Mr. Snap's car was located about 100 feet from the side door. They were walking swiftly to the car when a police officer yelled, "Hey, stop, no one is to leave this area." Mr. Snap told Rodney to get in a dark blue Chevrolet Monte Carlo SS and to let him handle the situation. Mr. Snap walked quickly to the police officer holding his badge out so that the Officer could see his credentials. As he got closer to the Officer, the officer noticed his credential and released the tension on his gun. Mr. Snap walked up to the officer and explained to him that Rodney was an international agent and he had to get to the airport for transport. He could not be caught up in this madness that went on inside. The police officer said, "I will have to get permission for you to leave through this back gate, I was told no one was to leave the compound. As the police officer turned to go to his car, Mr. Snap stabbed him in the neck with a box cutter that he retrieved out of his pocket and slid it halfway across his neck and held him close from behind. He could feel life slowly leaving his body as blood oozed down his uniform. Mr. Snap had to get him to the car before his body became too heavy. He held him close to his chest and walked him to the police car, opened the door and slowly placed the police officer in the front seat. There was so much noise, sirens, police, students screaming, that no one noticed the events that were going on at the back gate. Mr. Snap removed the box cutter from his throat, propped the body up and closed the door. He then walked over to the sidewalk where there was a wooded area and threw the box cutter into the woods. He swiftly ran back to the car, jumped in the driver's seat, made a U-Turn, went out the back gate and headed for "G" Street to cross the bridge to the airport.

Eugenia had her .22 cocked and ready; when she looked up and saw Brock hit the floor, Stephen hit the floor and Ila hit the floor all in a matter of seconds. Paula was standing still in a puddle of pee with tears running down her face. She saw the police and the fire department come running in, they must have been on campus because of the event and with all the students being there for the wedding. She slowly placed her .22 back into her ankle and pulled her badge out of her bra. She stood up slowly with her hands in the air to distract the officers from looking to the left. She told Paula to start screaming, Paula looked at Eugenia, saw the look in her eyes and started screaming at the top of her lungs. Eugenia looked to the left and saw Morris moving quickly to the back of the Chapel, but why was the camera man running towards him and guiding him out the back. She was sure that would all unravel later as she also knew that they were not the only people who worked for the Company at this wedding. She at this point did not know who to trust.

Anthony and his father were stunned, this was not the way things were supposed to go. "Shit" Anthony's father said. Anthony said, walk quickly down the aisle and see if she will let you help her. I am sure she wants to get out of all this mess. His father said, "Son you are brilliant." Anthony's father walked slowly to the front of the Chapel, asking the students who were left in Chapel if they were alright and he made it down to where Eugenia was standing. Paula was still screaming, and Eugenia wanted at this point to punch her in the face…. she could stop now, Morris was gone. But she went with it and walked slowly over to the pew and sat down. She looked over at Paula and mouthed, "OK enough." Paula slowly brought the scream to a sniffle. Paula walked over to the first pew and sat next to Eugenia. She was in total shock. Tears flowed from her eyes, she could not stop, her best friend was on the ground,

Brock was on the ground and the man who shot him was on the ground and the best man was gone. The best man looked so familiar, she wondered why she could not remember where she had seen him before. Slowly a very handsome man came up to her and wondered if she was alright, she shook her head yes and he went on to speak to Eugenia to see if she was alright. He took a seat beside Eugenia and said, "Would you like to get out of here, we could be husband and wife. You can give the police a statement and a number where you can be reached and show them whatever credentials you have, and we get out of here." Eugenia said, "Who are you?" Jerome said, "Superman, I have come to save you and keep you from being dragged down to the station and strip searched and they find that gun on your ankle and…." Eugenia said, "Let's walk." Jerome got up, pulled Eugenia up off the pew and they walked up the far-right aisle which did not have as much activity going on as everyone had run out or was settled on the left side of the Chapel where all the bodies were on the ground. At the end of the row of pews was a security guard from the school. He looked at Eugenia and knew she was on staff at the school. Eugenia told the security guard that she was going to the bridal dressing room to recover her things and that she would give the police officers a statement before she left the building. He shook his head and let them pass his check point. They walked slowly to the bridal dressing room. Eugenia closed the doors slowly and changed into her street clothes. Jerome stood there trying not to look but she was beautiful, just as beautiful as the night she placed handcuffs on him in S.E. DC fifteen years ago. She was a rookie cop whose testimony was the bullet that placed him into the prison system for fifteen years. It was very hard to find her, but he got to know some notable people while in prison as the crack epidemic was in full swing and many politicians and politically connected people had gotten caught up in drugs. Jerome went to prison with connections. He had been one of the largest drug dealers in S.E. DC and had many people in the system that he had employed and had taken really good care of their families while they did the time that he should have gotten. But on this night, Jerome had done something that he normally did not do and that was to try the product. He had a strict rule that only the women could try the product first. The women's critique of the product would place the price of the product and its purity. He had a great source, but he was like the Roman Kings, he did not try the product until someone else had tried it. He had set up his organization in Anacostia, which was in S.E. DC. His operation was run out of the Barry Farm housing project. It was a housing neighborhood that was built back in the 1950s for the working-class Whites, who eventually took flight as Black families were integrated into the neighborhood.

Eugenia was completely dressed and was trying to figure out how she and Jerome were going to get out of the dressing room without having to answer a thousand questions. There was a knock at the door. It opened slowly and there he was Eugenia's Prince George's police officer friend Officer Waters. He slowly closed the door. He looked at Eugenia and mouthed, "Are you OK?" Eugenia shook her head yes. Jerome could feel his palms start to sweat; this certainly was not part of his plan. How the hell was he going to get out of this. The officer told

Eugenia, "I am going to place handcuffs on both of you and lead you out of the building. Do you have your car"? Eugenia replied, "Yes but one of the men on the floor in the chapel who is dead has the keys in his pockets and he parked the car. I have no idea where it is." Officer Waters replied, "Let's now worry about that then, turn around and let me place handcuffs on both of you." Eugenia wondered why he had two sets of handcuffs and started to smile. He was probably going to stop by her apartment after the wedding, so he had an extra pair. All she could do was smile. Officer Waters looked at Jerome and said, "Eugenia who is your friend." Eugenia replied, "He is a friend of Ila's who helped me get out of the chapel into this room." Officer Waters looked at Jerome and said, "Do we know each other?" Jerome replied, "No I live out of town my son goes to school here and was invited to the wedding by Ms. Montgomery." Officer Waters said, "Turn around and let me put these handcuffs on you." Jerome turned around slowly, and beads of sweat started pouring down his face. The Officer could feel his tension. He said, "Relax man, I promise to take them off of you when we get off the campus." Jerome just shook his head. Eugenia assumed the position and he placed handcuffs on her. Officer Waters said, "Put everything you need in a bag, I will have one of the security guards come in and clean up the room." Eugenia said, "Paula has several items in this room also and she is still down front sitting on the first pew to the left." Officer Waters opened the door looked into the chapel and turned back around and said, "There is no one sitting on the pew, as a matter of fact the chapel is pretty much empty chapel except for police officers, medics, the medical examiner and a forensic officer a couple of people who look like students and police photographer." He said, "Gather your stuff, we are walking swiftly out the door." Eugenia gathers her stuff into the bag her tennis shoes were in and readied herself to be taken out the door. Officer Waters placed both in front of him and headed towards the door on the side of the building. Every officer he encountered he said taking the witnesses to the station. They walked swiftly to his police car, and he placed them both in the back seat.

Anthony was looking at the door of the bridal room. He had been asked to stand to the far left of the building. All that excitement had made him hungry. He wondered what they were going to do with all the food. Anthony saw the police officer enter the room; he knew his father was shitting in his pants right about now. He would wait patiently to see what happened next. He saw one of the security guards sneak some mini sandwiches. His stomach was growling but he knew there was no way he was going to take his eyes off the door. It took about 15 minutes for the door to open. The police officer was looking down to the front of the chapel. Anthony wondered what was going on. The officer went back into the room and came out with his father and Eugenia in handcuffs. "Shit" he said in his head. He walked slowly to the side door, gave the police officer standing at the door his name and phone number and showed his student ID. He said that a detective would be calling him for detailed information on what he saw within 48 hours. He walked out into the parking lot slowly not wanting to seem in a rush. He looked for the car and started walking towards it when two black sedans drove and four men, two black and two white got out of the car in suits, flashing badges and demanding to see the officer or detective in charge. The first man had a bag. He pulled out yellow crime scene tape and streamed it along the front of the door. Anthony decided not to stay around any longer, plus his father and Ms. Eugenia were being placed in the police cruiser, he had to follow them if he could. He then ran to the car and waited for the cruiser to pull off. The cruiser pulled off slowly. He waited ten seconds before he pulled out behind them. He felt for some reason he would not be taking them to the police station. Anthony did not want to get caught following them. As they entered the entrance to the college there was a patrol stop. "Shit" what was he going to tell the Officers. The cruiser pulled off of course no problem. Think, think, think. He came to a stop in front of the officers. "Roll down your window please," the officer said. "License and registration," the officer said. Anthony said, "Officer, my father was a witness to the tragedy that just took place at the college, and I am following the cruiser so that my father will have a ride home after he gives the officer his account of what happened in the chapel." The officers looked at each other, the second officer said, "Did you leave your name and contact phone number with one of the officers at the scene." Anthony replied, yes, but I was in the car waiting for my father. We were running late so I dropped him off and just decided to stay in the car. I really did not want to go to any old people's wedding." The second officer replied. "Officer Waters is probably taking them to the 3rd District Station on V Street, hurry young man you may be able to catch them." Anthony thanked the officers and drove slowly away. Damn It! He thought that was long enough to lose sight of the Cruiser. Fortunately for Anthony there was so much traffic, the cruiser was stuck at the light on "O" street. He drove very slowly and tried his best to stay behind the cruiser. The cruiser started to slow down, and Anthony knew the Officer was taking them to Eugenia's apartment. Anthony made a quick right to the back alley, turned off his lights and slowly moved down the alley. He and his dad had sat in the alley many days just watching the activities of Eugenia. It finally dawned on him that this was the police officer that spent so much time at Eugenia's apartment. Anthony laughed, of course he would not be taking her to jail, but what about his father. He eased halfway down the alley and turned off the engine. There was a set of trees that had a slight hole and that hole allowed him to look at the back of the apartment. Ms. Montgomery's apartment you could go into from the front, but Eugenia's apartment could only be entered through the back.

It was still and silent in the cruiser. Eugenia decided to make sure all her conversation with the officer was professional. "Officer Waters," she said, "Will you be taking us to the 3rd District station. I need to find a way back home after you have taken our accounts of what happened. Officer Waters replied, "Ms. Eugenia I am taking you to your apartment, what shall we do with you little friend." Eugenia looked at Jerome and said, "I am sure he can catch the subway down on Wisconsin Avenue and find his way back home wherever that is." Officer Waters replied, "Is that alright with you Sir, as it seems you have no other choice unless you really want me to take you to the Third District station and you can call someone from there." Jerome was silent for just a second and said, "No officer, if you will drop me off wherever you are taking this lovely lady, I will find my way home." Jerome thought he had no idea where Anthony Pierce Hollis might be, but he was his son and knew the game. Somehow, they would connect, in the meantime, he would act like he was walking toward the subway. His son's apartment was not far from Eugenia's. They inched down "O" street as it was New Year's Eve, and the traffic was heavy. It took 10 minutes just to get two blocks. Officer Waters could finally see the driveway to the apartment. He inched forward and made a right into the driveway and made the bend into the back of the building. He drove almost to the back alley and backed up to the steps to Eugenia's apartment. He sat for a moment, reached into the glove compartment for a pad and reached down into the console for a pen. "Sir what did you say your name was again," Waters said. Jerome hesitated and said, "Ancil Rogers". Mr. Rogers, please provide your phone number so that the detectives can call you and get a complete statement. Jerome thought fast, "703-845-4030," he said. Jerome looked at Eugenia and said, "I hope you are alright, please get my phone number from Officer Waters if I can assist you in any way." Waters looked in the back seat quickly, looked at him and then at Eugenia. He then quickly turned around and opened his door. He walked to the back of the car, opened the back door and assisted Jerome out of the back seat. He took the keys to the handcuffs out of his pocket and unlocked them. Jerome shook his hands and had a flashback of the day he got locked up in shackles and handcuffs. He would make this Bitch pay for the many years he spent in prison. Officer Waters said, "please find yourself away from this address. I will be here awhile if you decide to circle back, it would not be a good idea." Jerome looked at his punk ass and the words were on the tip of his tongue. He turned to Officer Waters and said, "You will not have to worry about that." Jerome proceeds to walk up the long driveway, not looking back. Officer Waters turned off the cruiser, walked over to the other back door and helped Eugenia get out of the car. Eugenia stood waiting to have her handcuffs taken off, but Officer Waters reached into the back of the cruiser, picked up her bags and locked the door. "Where are the keys to your apartment?" Eugenia said, "Are you not going to take these handcuffs off me? Waters laughed and said, "No." Eugenia gave him a glare and said, "The keys are in my jean pocket on the left side." He stood behind her and slid his hand into her jean pocket and gently retrieved the keys. Bags in one hand and his hands on her handcuffs he led her to the steps to her apartment. Eugenia walked to the steps and took them one at a time. She knew he would not be leaving. Her first thought was to get to the top of the steps back head butt him and go for her .22. Then she remembers, this man was the father of her child. She began to laugh in her head. When they got to the top of the stairs he let go of the handcuffs and requested Eugenia step aside while he placed the key in the door. Eugenia looked around quickly and she felt something in the air. She looked around slowly. Waters looked at her and said, "Don't worry that sorry mother fucker is not coming back, you are all mines tonight." Eugenia looked at him and said. "I have been through a lot tonight; can we have fun later in the week." Officer Waters said, "I just risk my damn job for you and all you can think about is what you have been through. Tonight I am going to work the tension out of your ass, and you are going to suck my dick till it burns. Are we clear?" Eugenia glared at him and looked down to see his dick getting hard. He opened the door slowly and told her to stay on the steps. He dropped the bags inside the door and leaned against the wall to check the bathroom, then he went across the hall and checked the bedroom. Checked the closets and walked back into the hallway. Slowly he went through the entire apartment to make sure it had not been compromised. He proceeded to turn on the lights and headed back to the front door to get Eugenia and the bags. He picked up the bags and opened the door wide so Eugenia could come inside. Once inside he closed and locked the door. Eugenia stood at the door wondering when he was going to uncuff her. Waters took the bags into the bedroom and walked back and grabbed Eugenia's arm and led her to the bedroom. Told her to sit on the side of the bed. Eugenia sat down and knew that the best thing to do was to let this story play out. The sooner he got his way, the sooner he would leave. Officer Waters went to the kitchen and placed double shots of Hennessy into glasses with two cubes of ice to take the sting away. He laughed as he walked down the hall with the drinks. Eugenia was being very obedient, which he loved. She knew just how to treat her man. He walked over to Eugenia, placed the drinks on the floor and asked her to stand up. Eugenia stood up. "Turn around," he said. Eugenia turned around. He slowly took the cuffs off and placed them on the floor with the drinks along with the key. Eugenia turned around and he told her to sit back down on the bed. He picked up her drink and handed it to her. He bent over and proceeded to take off her silver boots that were indeed killing her just like Ila said they would. He placed the boots to the side. He unclipped the twenty-two on her ankle and walked it over to the dresser. Eugenia was exhausted but was starting to feel her pussy jump. She decided to take control of the situation, or they would be there all night and she was concerned for Ila, wanted to cry for Brock and Stephen and wondered where the hell Morris went and who the fuck was the camera man. Her head was swirling.

Eugenia stood up and slowly unbuttoned her jeans and pulled down the zipper. She placed the drink back on the floor and took her jeans and panties off and left them on the floor. She walked over to the nightstand where she left his favorite toy and picked up the baby oil bottle from the nightstand. She walked over to the side of the bed and continued to take her clothes off. She felt that she was not smelling particularly good after sweating through all the gunfire, being on the ground, etc. Waters looked over at her and began to take off his uniform, placing all his firearms on the dresser. She took her blouse and bra and laid it in the chair. He came from the other side of the room, stood in front of her and grabbed her neck and began kissing her passionately. He had left all the lights on so there was no hiding his swollen dick. He began running his one hand up and down her body. He stopped as he slid his hand towards her pussy. With his hand still around her neck he said, "It seems you have gained a little weight; you are not pregnant are you." Eugenia's feet went cold. Eugenia said, "Don't be silly, with all this wedding preparation, I have not been exercising and all we have been doing is eating. I almost did not fit into the dress that was sized for me some time ago. Don't worry, I will be back to running and exercising soon. But can we talk about what you came in on for a moment and what you believe happened in the chapel." He looked at Eugenia and said, "I don't give a fuck what happened in that chapel, all I know is that you are alive, and Ila has been taken to the hospital by now and I don't give two shits about everyone else." Eugenia could feel his grip on her neck get tighter. She decided to take control. "Take your Bitch hands off my neck and get on your knees and suck my pussy." He slowly released the grip on her neck and sat on the side of the bed and pulled her to him. He leaned back and told her to bend her knees and sit on his face. He eased her on top of his face, and she bent over so that her knees locked his head, and her arms and elbows were on the bed. He took both hands and opened her pussy with ease knowing exactly where her clitoris was, he found it and locked on sucking on it as if he was sucking on a straw. It took her all of three minutes to come all over his face. He took the bed covers and wiped his face and continued. Eugenia began to sweat; she could feel her legs start to shiver and at that point he moved her down, turned her over, grabbed her by the legs and placed them over his shoulders and began kissing her body. He licked her breast with precision and began kissing her body until he got to her stomach. He looked up at her and said, "If you are pregnant with my child, your lifestyle is going to change drastically." He continued down to her pussy, opened the lips and sucked hard until Eugenia had tears in her eyes. After coming so much that the bed covers were wet, he got up, moved her down to the end of the bed and grabbed her arms so that she would be in a sitting position. He went and grabbed the drinks from the floor. Gave Eugenia her drink and he threw his drink back quickly. Eugenia took a swallow of her drink and placed the glass on the floor. She grabbed his dick and placed it full into her mouth while grabbing his balls. Once in her mouth, she did small bites all the way down the shaft of his dick. She could fill his dick swelling up as she sucked it hard with full thrust. She took her right hand and placed it on the entrance of his ass hole to see if it was moist. She knew he could not wait for his toy. She pulled his dick out of her mouth, stood up and got behind him. She began rubbing her hand between the crack of his ass. He moaned. She slowly pushed him to the side of the bed and told him to bend over. He bent over and Eugenia picked the baby oil up from the nightstand, uncapped it and poured it down the crack of his ass. She slowly rubbed the oil on his ass and began to slap him hard. He grabbed his dick and began to caress it slowly. Eugenia grabbed his hand and poured baby oil into it to assist with his masturbation. She placed the baby oil back on the dresser and picked up the toy and put it on the first setting, slid it down his ass until she could feel his butt open to receive the toy that pleased him more than pussy. She placed the toy in his ass, and she could feel him untense. She slowly entered his ass and began moving the toy in and out. Once his ass was well lubricated, she turned it to the setting number five and pounded his ass until he screamed like a hurt animal. "Stop," he said. Eugenia said, "No" and jammed the toy so far up his ass he fell forward. "Put your knees up," Eugenia commanded. He slowly got up on his knees and Eugenia again placed the toy up into the cavity of his ass. He was moving like a horse, getting into a slow circular motion to make sure he got the entire pleasure out of this experience. Eugenia began slapping him across the ass and called him names. He screamed louder. She was ready to end this. She pulled the toy out of his ass and placed it on the nightstand. She slid back first under him until they were looking each other in the eye. She placed her legs around his neck and slowly put the head of his penis into her swollen pussy. She played with the head for approximately five minutes and then grabbed his ass so that his entire penis was surrounded in the shaft of her pussy. He humped about ten times and cried out as he exploded so much semen that it came out of her pussy before he pulled out. He pulled out slowly and fell over onto the bed. Instantly there was deep breathing. She laid there and listened to the snores of the man that would be the father of her child. Her body was emotionally weak, it did not take her long to fall asleep. It seemed they had been sleeping for hours, but as her beeper went off and his beeper went off, they both sat straight up.

Officer Riley Bridges who lived in the basement of Ila and

Paula's apartment building was the first police officer at the altar as he was standing in the back of the Chapel. He had not taken a seat because he was on duty and did not know how long he could stay. When he heard the first gun shots, he looked outside the side door believing it was coming from outside, then he saw the groom collapse in front of the Chapel and then he heard another gunshot from a larger weapon and saw another man fall. He unclipped his gun and started running to the front of the Church with other security personnel but kept running into students who were trying their best to get out of the Chapel. The once beautiful aisle to the front of the Church was filled with people and felt like it was a football field long to get to the front. Officer Bridges got to the front of the Chapel and looked over at Paula and she mouthed, "Get the big gun." He looked at the gun lying next to the man with a bullet wound in the front of his head. The security guards were hovering around Ila and pulling her away from the carnage as she had hit the floor. They were trying to see if Ila had been hit by a bullet. Officer Riley Bridges walked slowly over to the body of the man shot in the head and picked up the Glock. He placed this Glock in his back and walked over to Paula. He told Paula to "Get up," he grabbed her by the elbow and walked her to the left side of the Church, as the right side was beginning to fill up with EMTs, and police officers. The door to the left side led to the choir room. He looked around for another exit and there was another door to the left side of the room. Bridges opened the door slowly and decided to draw the shooter's gun and not his own just in case he had to drop someone. He looked both ways down the hallway, it was empty. This was a huge school, with many doorways, hallways, and buildings. He decided to make a right that would lead to the back-parking lot of the Chapel. He grabbed Paula's hand and felt something. A slight spark. It confused him as Paula had been his neighbor for many years and he had never given her a second thought. He did think she was lovely, and she had a big juicy ass, but... off limits because of her man Drew. He shook his head and grabbed her hand firmly to let her know not to let go. They swiftly walked down the hallway and turned right as his police car was parked behind another police car. That officer was on patrol while the ceremony was going on. He had pulled up behind him and parked his car. He left the keys in the car and had asked the officer to look out while he went into the Chapel. The Officer said, "No problem." Riley walked up the sidewalk, opened the side Chapel door and entered. He made conversation with the security officers and the EMTs that were hanging outside. He had gotten there late as he had been assigned to assist the investigation of two men found in a hotel room. The scene in that hotel room was like something out of a horror movie. It was definitely a hit. No fingerprints were lifted, the only thing they got prints from was the cassette player. That was the only thing they were hoping could help crack the case. But when he left the scene, the CSI people were just getting started. He loved being an Officer in the Metro area. There was never a dull moment. They walked swiftly to his patrol car. He opened the back-seat door for Paula and she quickly got in. He walked swiftly up to the other patrol officer's car to thank him and to tell him he was taking one of the witnesses to the station. He was surprised that the Officer was sitting in the car. He walked around the car to the driver's side and as he got close, he could smell blood. It was an instinctive smell that you could capture right away after being so many years on the job. He walked up to the window and there he was with a large slice in his throat, his head dangled from his shoulders. He decided not to call it in as he did not want Paula to be in the middle of yet another investigation. His stomach got weak. He ran to the sidewalk and ran swiftly to the grass and threw up. When you know you are going to a crime scene, you mentally prepare yourself but walking up on an officer like that with his throat cut, was something you could never prepare for. He wiped his mouth with the sleeve of his uniform and ran to his patrol car, jumped in the driver's side, backed up slightly and turned around headed toward the back gate. By this time, there were two other officers at the back gate. He drove up slowly, rolled down his window and told them that he was taking a witness to the station as they were trying to get as many people out of the crime scene area as possible. They both shook their heads. He looked over at their patrol cars and they were Alexandria police. Great they would have no idea who he was, unless one was smart enough to take his tag number. He did not think they were that smart.

Rodney did not question Mr. Snap or his motive for killing the police officer. He just wanted to make the last transport out of National Airport. He was keeping his eye on this man. He did know the password, but that did not mean he was a U.S. operative. "Damn It," all his things are at the hotel Rodney thought to himself. He had the key in his breast pocket. Rodney said, "Man I need to go by the hotel and get our items out of the hotel room." Mr. Snap replied, "Where were you staying?" "Georgetown Inn." Rodney replied. Mr. Snap made a quick right onto "O" Street and as quickly as possible got to Wisconsin Avenue. It seemed they caught every light. Rodney was hoping that Mr. Snap would turn on WHUR, but he did not seem like the type to listen to WHUR. He just sat in silence wanting to get his belongings and getting to the airport in time to take the last transport. Rodney's stomach started to churn. He was not sure whether his best friend was dead or alive. He did not know if Ila had survived as all he remembers was seeing her hit the floor. "Please pull over," Rodney screamed. Mr. Snap pulled over quickly. Rodney opened the door and hurled. It seemed to be a continuous gut-wrenching vomit that hurt his stomach as it entered his throat and burned as it landed in his mouth and then onto the ground. Again, and again. Finally, there was nothing left in his stomach. He pulled the handkerchief from his tuxedo jacket and wiped his mouth. He slowly closed the door of the car and leaned his head back. Mr. Snap put the car and gear and continued down "O" street. He drove up to the front of the hotel and Rodney jumped out. There was nowhere to park. It was New Year's Eve. The valet person was giving him the eye. He slowly drove the car up to the valet person. He showed the valet his badge. He waved him to park on the side of the entrance where the yellow strip was located. He slowly moved the car down the driveway and waited for Rodney. Mr. Snap rolled down the windows to get fresh cold air into the Monte Carlo as much as he had done it, it was never easy to kill someone, you always left a piece of your humanity with every kill. He sat in the car listening to the traffic and the party goers and thought, one day he would be able to enjoy a life that included parties, celebrations, birthdays, and holidays. He had decided many years ago that the Company would be his life's journey but in some respects that decision he made so many years ago was made by a young man who felt the United States was the only place in the world where a man could truly be free, but in time it was clear that being free was a state of mind and not a reality in the United States. He drifted back to his time at the Academy and how he wanted to be an operative then, but his knowledge of computers and Computer Aided Design (CAD), placed him in the halls of headquarters for more than 15 years. He finally drew an assignment to find an operative named Maurice Glover. The only problem with the assignment was by the time he found Glover; he was already dead in a hotel room. He was hoping to talk to Ila, Paula, or Eugenia after the wedding at the reception to get some additional intel on Maurice. Like what was he doing in the hotel room and who was the man he was found with. He finally found out Maurice was staying in Ila's old apartment but had no idea how he ended up at the Marriott Hotel in Crystal City Virginia.

Rodney ran to the elevator. He did not know what he was going to do with Brock's items. He decided to just put all of Brock's items in his suitcase in the hope that he survived the gunshot wounds and one day he would return all the items to his friend. The door opened on his floor. He ran down the hall, pulled the key card out of his breast pocket and opened the door. He felt his stomach churn again. He ran into the bathroom and hurled into the toilet. All that was left was liquid and a burning acid reflux in his stomach. He had to pull himself together. There were complimentary nuts at the bar. He broke open the jar, poured a handful in his hand and popped them all in his mouth. He chewed very slowly so that they would be a coating for his stomach. He walked to the bathroom chewing the nuts and grabbed a glass filled it with water and chased the nuts down. He stood for a moment and looked in the mirror. Time had been good to him. He was still a very handsome man, but he lived a life of nerve ending assignments. He did not have time to walk down that yellow brick road. He pulled himself together and started cleaning up the bathroom. He took Brock's mouthwash and emptied it onto a washcloth. He placed the cap back on the mouthwash and placed it in the garbage can. He did not know if he or Brock had touched the complimentary soap, so he threw that away from both bathrooms. He began wiping down the doorknobs, faucet knobs, liquor bottles, glasses, anything that a fingerprint could be left on. He took the laundry bag out of the closet and placed all Brock's belongings in the bag including his shoes. There was no need to take his belongings with him. He would ask Mr. Snap to destroy them. He packed up his toiletries and clothing and placed it in his suitcase. He decided to leave a note for maids to help themselves to the liquor. Only a couple of shots had been taken out of each bottle. He went around the room one more time with the washcloth, took all the trash bags from the bathroom and bedroom and placed it in the laundry bag with Brock's items and pulled the string. He looked around the room one last time and remembered to place his card key in the laundry bag. He picked up his suitcase, the laundry bag and the washcloth and headed for the door. He stopped as his senses felt like something was being left behind. He walked around the rooms again. Found nothing, decided he was wasting a lot of precious time. He looked down and had forgotten he still had a tuxedo on. He did not have time to unpack his suitcase again and change, he was going to have to get to the transport. He thought the last transport was a 10:00 p.m. He could just make it, it was 9:00 p.m. He stood at the door and still something was wrong. He could not spend any more time. He took the cloth and opened the door. The door automatically closed on its own. As he walked swiftly down the hall, he dropped the washcloth in a trash can at the elevator. He pushed the button for the elevator, and it seemed to take forever. He had started to sweat and remembered that he had not eaten anything, and his blood sugar was probably dropping fast. The elevator door opened and of course it was filled with celebrating people. He eased on quietly and got in the back of the elevator. People on the elevator were singing "Billie Jean" by Michael Jackson for some unknown reason. He just stood quietly in the back of the elevator until it came to the ground floor. He let all the celebrators get off and he walked off last. He made a left from the elevator and headed to the front door.

Mr. Snap looked at his watch, it had been about 15 minutes. He should be headed towards the front door. He wanted to get a picture of Rodney just in case he needed it later while researching the case of Maurice Glover. He had a feeling all the players at the wedding were intricately involved with

Maurice. He slowly pulled away from the no parking zone and pulled around slowly so that he could see the front door. He pulled his camera from the back seat and took the flash off. He did not want the flash to go off as he took Rodney's picture as he was coming out of the hotel. He looked up and there he was. He took three quick pictures as he stood at the front door looking for the car. He soon saw the car and started walking towards the car. He quickly placed the camera on the floor of the back seat. As Rodney came toward the car, he mouthed, "Pop the trunk." Mr. Snap reached into the glove box and popped the trunk and Rodney placed all the items in the trunk. He walked to the passenger side door and opened it up slowly. He took a long look at Mr. Snap as he wanted to be able to draw every feature of his face once he got on the transport. Once seated he nodded his head and Mr. Snap pulled off. The traffic was crazy as the revelers for New Years were everywhere. They slowly crossed the Frances Scott Key bridge and headed to the airport. Traffic was thick and moving slowly. Time was ticking. Rodney's heart began to beat fast, and he began to sweat even more. When they got to the middle of the bridge, Rodney's heart felt like it was going to jump out of his chest. He had a flashback of crossing the 14th Street Bridge on that fateful day that Air Florida hit the 14th street bridge. It was cold, snow was falling fast and there was a weird fog coming from the Potomac River. He was following the love of his life across the bridge to spend the evening and probably the last evening together as he was being transferred to California. He could see Ila's car in front of him about ten cars down. Then for some reason the traffic stopped, and you could see a blue and white airplane not lifting as it was supposed to, people began backing up on the bridge and backing up fast. It was incredible the number of cars that got off to the end of the bridge before the plane hit wheels first into the bridge. There were so many more who did not make it across, cars started to explode, people were screaming. Rodney turned off the car, holstered his gun, took all his personal belongings out of the car, and placed them in his backpack. Took his small tool kit out of the backpack, got out of the car, removed the licensed plate, placed the plate in his backpack and began to walk back towards DC. Cars, people sirens, screams, fire, people in the water screaming for help. He closed all of that out and kept walking. He walked to the end of the bridge and made a right. He was looking for a phone booth. He walked what seemed like ten miles. He turned onto Ohio Drive and saw signs to U.S. Park Police station. He walked an additional three miles and walked up to the complex guard and requested entrance with his credentials. They immediately opened the gate and offered him assistance. One of the guards walked Rodney to the main building where he was granted entrance. He was escorted to a meeting room. He was soaked to the bone. The guard requested that he go to the men's room and remove his clothing and they would get a uniform, shoes, and socks for him to wear. He thanked him. He did not care if the uniform was a perfect fit, he just wanted to get out of those clothes. He stood in the bathroom cried out Ila's name and began to cry with no control. He screamed her name out loud. How could this happen? The guard entered the bathroom and just left the clothes, shoes, socks, underwear, and a coat on the chair.

"Rodney," "Rodney," Mr. Snap said. Rodney looked over at him as he totally forgot for a few minutes where he was. "We are at the airport and the transport leaves in 15 minutes, we are going to the back gate. Show your credentials that should be enough to get you to the transport." Rodney nodded his head in acknowledgement. "Snap," Rodney said, "There is a laundry bag full of items that I need you to get rid of in the trunk. He nodded his head in acknowledgement. They pulled up to the back gate, Snap showed his credentials and Rodney showed his. The gates opened slowly. He could see the activity at the transport. There was another gate just ahead. The car could not go through this gate. They pulled up slowly and showed their credentials. Rodney jumped out of the car and ran around to the trunk to get his suitcase. Snap popped the trunk. Rodney grabbed his suitcase, closed the trunk, and walked swiftly through the gate. Once through the gate, he looked back at the Monte Carlo and at Snap. He wanted to take a picture in his mind of the car and the man for the last time. He then went into a full trot to get to the transport. There was yet another gate. He had to declare his firearm which was in the suitcase unloaded. He had dropped the Glock at the wedding. In hindsight that was probably not a good idea, but it was instinct. *The Godfather* "Drop the gun, keep the cannoli." He had to smile to himself at that reference. The guards rechecked his credentials, gave him his suitcase and he ran to the steps of the transport. He turned around one more time and saw the lights blink on the Monte Carlo. He ran up the steps and was met by the military flight attendant. He took his bag and secured it in a cage in the front of the plane. There were only six people on the plane. They exchanged head nods but nothing else. He found a window seat. He began to take his tuxedo jacket off and felt something. He reached into the pocket and there it was Ila's and Brock's ring box. He held the box tight for a moment and placed it back into the pocket. He sat in the seat, placed the jacket in the seat next to him. The military attendant came down the aisle to tell everyone to secure all items, they had just gotten clearance to take off. As the plane slowly made its way to the main runway, it made a slow right and began to pick up speed. As the plane began to ascend, tears flowed down Rodney's cheeks because once again he did not know if Ila or Brock were dead.

Ila could feel herself dropping to the floor screaming Brock's name. Her head hit the floor hard. She could hear the noise, sirens, smell the people around her and then nothing, the next voice she heard was her father's. "Ila, Ila where are you, I am ready to go to the store." Ila came skipping down the steps of the home that her family lived in. She knew that they were not going to go to the store just yet, but they would walk in the alleyway to the Johnson Brothers Auto Body garage, and he would gamble for about 30 minutes. Ila's Father could really roll dice. Ila called their dog Victor, who fell in line behind them as they made their way to the alley. There was not a day they went to the garage where he did not come out $10.00 richer. That meant we could get the necessary groceries, ice cream and beer for her dad. Ila was the lookout for the police.

She would sit on the hood of a 1962 Chevy so that she could look both ways down the alley. Victor would sit at the back end of the car waiting for Jack, her father, to move again. The police never came down the alley, but occasionally, a rookie would make his way down the alley and try to start asking questions. If Ila saw the police she would start singing "Mary Had a Little Lamb.," very loud. Suddenly, all the guys were in cars, looking under hoods, and picking up oil cans. This day, Ila was enjoying her chips and pop when she saw the police car coming down the alley. She started singing very loud and saw the guys move quickly into their respective spots. Ila continued to sit on the hood and as the police slowly drove by, she was instructed to wave and say hello very loudly. The patrol car drove very slowly past the shop but did not stop. It made a right out of the alley onto the main road which was Brushton Avenue. The guys waited about five minutes because rookies were known to double back. Ila had finished her chips and pop. Her Father had won his $10.00 and was ready to leave. One of the guys drew a blade and told Jack that he needed to spend a little more time at the garage so that he could have a chance to win his money back. Ila was sitting on the Chevy thinking, this guy must be new if he thought he could draw a blade on her father. Jack placed his fingers in his mouth and whistled for Victor. He came around the corner ready for battle. Victor, a very large brown and black German shepherd, jumped on the man from the back. Giving Jack enough time to grab the knife out of the man's hand. Victor was biting the back of the man's neck and it started to bleed. Jack whistled again in short sets and Victor left the man on the ground and ran and stood by Ila's father. The man slowly got up bleeding and walked slowly to his car which was down the alley slightly. One of the Johnson Brothers came out of the garage with a shotgun and stood at the garage at the ready in case this crazy man was going to his car for a gun. The man was bleeding so bad, even if he had a gun, he was in no condition to try to use it. Suddenly, all the guys came out of the garage and stood. The man made a U-turn and fled the alleyway. Mr. Johnson said the guy was from East Liberty and did not know the rules. You lose, you lose. They all started to laugh. Jack gave the "Mason" handshake to Mr. Johnson, and we walked off down the alley headed towards the store. Ila had to sit outside on a crate with Victor until her father came out of the store. He came out with two arms filled with groceries in brown paper bags. They looked heavy, but the store was only three blocks away and her father was used to carrying that load. Ila skipped along with Victor talking twenty miles an hour talking about what happened in the alley. Her father stopped cold and said, "You mention one word of what when on to your mother and your adventures with me are over, are we clear." Ila looked at her father and replied "Clear." They walked the rest of the way in silence. Halfway home he stopped, put the bags on the ground and pulled out a package of beef jerky. He gave the long stick to Ila so that she and Victor could share on the way home. Ila started to skip and so did Victor, they were so happy to get a treat. As they turned the corner onto Mulford Street, it was like turning the corner to Oz. Kids were playing in the street, grandmothers and grandfathers on the porch, junkies in the apartment building on the corner sitting outside and a huge hopscotch in the middle of the street. Ila and Victor ran down the street to the house. Victor ran up on the porch and Ila ran out to the street to play hopscotch. Jack was so proud to have a home for his family. Even though it was a bit crowded, as his wife Lorraine's mother and father lived there along with a child that Lorraine's mother had had late in life. But all in all, it was one big happy family. He bound the stairs and entered the house. Ila's mother looked at all the groceries and never said a word as she knew how much money he left the house with. She grabbed one of the bags and headed towards the kitchen. Ila's father had done his duty, he was headed to the porch to smoke and drink a beer and wait for dinner.

The EMTs and security personnel at the University were all in shock. Nothing like this had ever happened at the University. There was so much going on they had a tough time getting all the people who might have been involved together. And because of who was getting married, there were police from Maryland, DC, and Virginia. Agent Carlton Watson had been assigned to the wedding as there were several operatives at the wedding and Rodney had flown in on a transport from California to attend and be the best man. There were too many operatives involved with this wedding not to have people here to make sure things did not go south and south they went. He could not believe he was pretending to be a photographer. He had taken up photography as a hobby, so he was very familiar with angles, lighting, and skin color and how lights affect the look you receive. He was taking pictures of the wedding party and tried his best to get shots from all angles of the Chapel just in case he needed them for his investigation into the death of Maurice. After he heard gunshots, he had to freeze his instincts to pull his gun, get next to a wall so that he could have a panorama of the entire chapel. He saw Rodney looking around for an escape route. He had been to the Chapel on more than one occasion just to get the layout so that he could be prepared for anything during the ceremony. But this was not what he expected. He walked swiftly towards the altar to make sure that Rodney got out of the Chapel before the cavalry arrived. Pretending to take pictures of the chaos and carnage, he walked up to Rodney and took him by the elbow and led him out of the Chapel.

As Ila ran to the street to play hopscotch, she could see Mr. Burns who always sat on the porch and watched little girls play and he always offered them candy. Ila was afraid of Mr. Burns, his eyes seemed to burn through her, she kept her distance. But her friends had told her that Mr. Burns would give them a dime and sometimes a quarter just to touch them, nothing else. They used to laugh about how he would pull his dick out and it looked like a worm that had gotten wet in the rain. They would all laugh. Ila wanted no part of Mr. Burns or his wet worm penis. She also understood that if her father found out Mr. Burns was asking to touch her, he would be spending the rest of his life in jail because he would kill him. So, Ila did not give Mr. Burns any reason to call her over to the porch. Her friends would go all the time to get the money to buy taffy apples and donuts from the stores up the street. Ila's friend Sharon went up on the porch all the time. She really liked spending time with Mr. Burns. She even went into his home. Sharon was one year older than Ila which made her fifteen years of age. Sharon had already started her period and she would sit around and talk to us about her period and how she had cramps and would throw up. We were all terrified to come on our periods.

It seemed like time flew by and all the girls came on their period at the same time. Ila over to the alley where the other girls were getting ready to walk to Belmar Gardens to watch the boys play basketball. She had her eyes on a young man named Christopher Baker. But all the girls had their eyes on Christopher Baker. But Ila felt he really had an eye for her. She had a small jar of Vaseline so she put some Vaseline on her lips so that they would shine. Her hair was long and braided in one large braid. Hoop earrings, tight jeans, 5-dollar tennis shoes that she washed every day and a t-shirt. They all shared the Vaseline and talked loudly and laughed. They took the long way so they could walk past Uncle Grady's barbershop. All the older guys hung out there and they loved running in saying hello to Uncle Grady and him telling them to get out of the barbershop right now. They would all run out laughing while looking at the older guys and wishing they could date them when they got older. The walk to Belmar Gardens was about 15 blocks or more, but talking and walking and putting on the Vaseline, the time went by extremely fast. Sharon had more chests than the rest of us and she made sure it was in full view when we went to the Basketball court. She on the other hand had her eyes on another young man, Paul Johnson. Ila was glad she did not like Christopher because with that chest and her experience Ila would not stand a chance. As we walked toward the courts, all the boys of course acted like they did not see us, but soon they were missing shots and screaming across the court at us. We loved it. We knew to sit close to the water fountain because eventually they would come to get some water. It did not take Christopher long to have someone take his place. He walked slowly off the court glistening and smiling as he walked towards the group of girls. Ila thought her heart would jump out of her chest as he walked about all the girls and stood in front of her and wiped off his sweat and took Ila's pop out of her hand that he knew she had saved it for him. They had stopped at the store right before they got to the court so they would all have something to drink as the boys came off the court. Soon after Christopher left the court the rest of the guys followed to get their gulps of pop or to drink from the water fountain, and soon the basketball game was over, and everyone had partnered up and was walking towards the swings or the benches to sit and talk. Christopher and Ila had only kissed. There was never any real touching, but she noticed when he came off the court that his penis was standing differently, that was probably why he wanted to move away from the crowd so fast. Ila laughed. She had no idea what to do if he asked her to touch it. She would have to ask her friend Sharon what to do as she told me she held Mr. Burns' penis for about 10 minutes for five dollars. She brought us all candy, chips, and soda that day. She told the other girls she got an allowance, but I knew differently.

The couples cuddled and kissed, and someone was sitting on the picnic table under the pavilion watching everything. It was a short distance from the basketball court, but we all stopped in our tracks when the music began to blast from the pavilion. The young man sitting under the pavilion had a boom box and he had turned the volume completely up. It did not take long for the girls to leave their puppy loves and start to dance. The boys just looked, none of them would join the girls on the grass. Ila knew they enjoyed seeing the girls jiggle and shake. Sharon came over and whispered in my ear. "You know who that is under the pavilion." Ila said, "No." Sharon started giggling, "That is Mickey. He is older than we are but girl he is fine." Ila looked over at the pavilion and could not make out the shadow that was sitting there playing music. Then he placed his "Namesake" song in the tape player. "Mickey's Monkey" by Smokey Robinson and the Miracles. You could see his figure stand up and begin to dance. Sharon lost her mind and began to dance and jiggle like someone on "American Bandstand." We all loved watching the show and making fun of how the young White people danced. That song even got the boys to start dancing and Mickey was imitating James Brown under the pavilion. Everyone broke out into the "Jerk," and each took a turn dancing inside a circle. Mickey played the song back-to-back, so everyone had a turn in the circle, and he had fun dancing by himself. Of course, we all had worked up a sweat and the girls now of course were worried about how their hair looked. Ila laughed because she had wonderful hair, she was blessed no matter what, it always looked good. She never worried about her hair but always worried about how she looked. The music stopped and Ila looked in the sky and realized that it was getting dark. Now there was one rule in Jack's house, and that was you better be home before the streetlights came on. Ila walked over to Christopher and told him she had to go. It was getting late. He only had to walk to the corner, and he would be home. All the girls had at least a 10-block walk. She kissed Christopher and walked around to all the girls to let them know it was time to go. Sharon was standing in front of Paul, rubbing his penis with her hand. Paul's eyes were in the back of his head. Ila walked over and whispered in the ear that it was time to go. She kissed Paul long and hard and walked away. We left the boys looking at us walking away and we swayed more than normal to make sure they would look at us until we were out of sight. As we turned the corner onto Brushton Avenue, we started to walk then run, because if we were late, we all would be on punishment. We dropped off the girls along the way and then we turned onto Mulford Street. It was like Mecca. Everyone was sitting on their porches and looking at their watches as we walked down the street and when Sharon and Ila got midway down the street the light came on. Ila ran up on the porch and Sharon ran down the street. Ila had not been on the porch for five minutes before her father came out on the porch to do a body check. I was the only one home on time. He started whistling through his teeth and fingers. I always marveled as to how he was able to do that. As his whistle got louder, I could see my brother and sister running down the street. They would have to do extra chores for being late. But truly

Jack was just glad to have his children at home and on the porch. When my brother and sister reached the house, my father pointed for them to go inside of the house. He looked down at Ila and said, "15 minutes and you bring your ass in the house." Ila nodded and was so glad she had made it home on time. And laughed out loud because it was usually her that would have to do more chores this time it was her siblings. About time. Too Funny.

Ila's father Jack was a hardworking man. He had to work two jobs to take care of his family. He did not want his wife to work, but to pay for the home that they desperately wanted for the family everyone had to chip in. Jack was not happy that there were so many people living in this house, but each person contributed to the payment of the mortgage. His wife's mother, father, and a son that his wife's mother had in midlife. So Troy was the uncle of his kids. Jack's wife's mother and her other daughter were at the hospital having babies at the same time. It made local and national news and all the newspapers. It is made for close quarters but is really made for a complete family. And it would not be forever. As he made additional money, he would be able to assist his wife's mother, father, and Troy to move into their own place. But for now, it was best for him and his family. He took the night shift at Westinghouse Electric, and his wife worked the early morning shift so that there was always someone home, including his wife's mother. After he worked from 11 p.m. to 7:00 a.m. would leave his job and for three days out of the week go to a drug store and clean it before it opened at 10:00 a.m. He would leave that job and go straight home. It would be 11:30

a.m. before he returned to the house. Grandma would be sitting on the porch swing. He would slowly get out of his beige Chrysler and walk slowly up the steps. His wife Lorraine was in a carpool and was already gone as her hours were 7:00 a.m. to 3:00 p.m. Grandma would look up and holler out, "Left you a little something to eat on the stove." Jack would blow her a kiss and walk into the house where in the vestibule lay his gray and black German Shepherd Victor. Victor jumped up to get his greeting rub and laid back down. For sure no one could come through the front or back door as Victor was vicious to people who were not a part of the family or extended family. Ila's friends would stand on the sidewalk and scream her name. They would never come up on the porch. He would hang his hat in the hallway, take off his work shoes and line them up against the wall where everyone's shoes would eventually be at the end of the day. He slowly walked to the kitchen to eat the delicious meal that grandma had cooked. Pot roast, browned potatoes, and green beans. And of course, a tall glass of red Kool-Aid with too much sugar. He ate slowly, savoring the flavors and trying not to fall asleep. The breeze from the back door being open was very pleasant. He knew if he sat too long after eating, he would fall asleep in the chair. He ate all his food, placed the dirty dishes in the sink, wiped off the table and dragged himself through the dining room to the stairs leading to the second floor. Their room was at the top of the stairs. He wanted to crawl right into bed but knowing all the cleaning chemicals his body came in contact, a bath was always in order. His wife had already drawn the water into the tub. He just had to turn on the hot water to warm it up. He stood in front of the mirror and glazed into the eyes of a man who had lost both of his parents, had spent four years in the Navy and met the love of his life and they soon had three children. He was surprised at how handsome he still was after all these years. Which was a blessing and a curse at the same time. He could not go to the corner bar without women making sure they were noticed and available. Yes, he had slipped on several occasions, but he always made it clear to those women that he was happily married and that whatever they had would be a one-night stand. He placed all his clothes into the dirty clothes hamper, turned on the hot water and slowly eased himself into the bathtub. It was not long before he drifted off while in the tub. His dreams were always about the time he spent on a submarine while in the Navy. He was one of the few Black men in the Navy and he was constantly fighting because the White boys always had some shit to say. But he knew if he did the four years, he would have VA benefits which included housing and he always wanted a home of his own.

Ila was always the first one up. She wanted to get to the bathroom before everyone else. There was only one bathroom and nine sometimes ten people had to use it daily. She washed up quickly as baths were taken the night before. She brushed her teeth, placed the blue magic grease in her hair, brushed it back into a ponytail with a rubber band and placed a piece of red ribbon she had brought with her allowance around the ponytail. She had a roller in the front of her hair for her bangs. She had laid out her clothes the night before on the chair in the bedroom that she shared with her sister. As she was leaving the bedroom her sister came down the hall. Her brother was always the last one to get up and he would be rushing to not be late for school. Ila used the common Vaseline. Legs, arms, face, feet, deodorant, then placed on clothes. Make sure oxfords were wiped off and socks were turned inside out because you had to wear them at least twice. Last look in the cracked stand-up mirror her dad had found on the street. But the crack was at the top of the mirror, so it served the purpose, and she was glad they had it, it felt glamorous. Like looking at the Doris Day show as she came down the spiral staircase as she sang "Que Sera Sera." Ila ran down the hallway to the stairs, bound the stairs two at a time and hit the landing. Grandma had already made lunches in brown paper bags, which we also used to cover our books. Ila attended a neighborhood school that was 95 percent Black. She loved going to school. The teachers cared about their students and were determined to make sure they were successful in school. Plus, we had a swimming pool so that everyone learned how to swim. She kissed her grandmother, grabbed her coat, lunch and books and petted Victor on the way out of the door and there they were her tribe of friends. We had many stops to make before school. To Mr. DeLeo's store to split donuts with the few pennies we had. Picked up Susanne as she lived closer to the school and of course picked up a boy or two along the way. This morning the air was clear but crisp. Mid-September weather was a teaser to the cold winter days ahead. Ila looked forward to all the seasonal changes. Each season brought surprises, some days off from school, pep rallies, football games, fall dances, etc. She was looking forward to finishing up her 9th grade year and moving on to high school. We all talked at once and the 10 block walk to school went by quickly. As we got close to the gates of the school, there he was *Mickey.* Sharon about peed in her pants. "There he is," Sharon said. I looked up, "Who, I said, "Mickey," she replied with a scream. She composed herself and we all walked by him slowly and gave him the head nod. Sharon screamed, "Thank you for the music the other day." He nodded his head as well and then he yelled "Ila, let me talk to you." Ila turned around and pointed to herself and shouted, 'You talking to me." He yelled, "That is your name right." Ila looked at Sharon and the rest of the tribe. Sharon looked like she could kick my head to Alaska, the rest were saying things in a whisper, he is too old for you, he is a bad boy, don't go over there. Ila looked at her friends and looked at Mickey and she said, "I will catch up with you guys at lunch." They all slowly walked away, and Ila walked back to the gate to see what Mickey had on his mind.

As she walked up to him Ila said, "How do you know my name?" Mickey replied, "Do I look like a man who does not know who all the pretty ladies are in the neighborhood." Of course, that is not what Ila thought he would say, she could feel her face becoming flush. "Don't blush," he said. Ila just looked at him and said, "What do you want?" He replied, "I want you to think about cutting school soon so you can spend the day with me." Ila replied, "So you cut school all the time." Mickey said, "I don't go to school any longer, I am about to go to the Service, but I want to get to know you before I leave." Ila stood there for a minute and replied, "I am going to miss roll call for my first class, I have got to go," She turned and started walking away. He yelled, "Think about what I said, it will be a day you will never forget." Ila started walking faster and was surprised that her panties had gotten wet like she had peed on herself. She started to run; she did not want to miss the bell. Once inside the school, she ran into the bathroom to make sure she had not peed on herself. She went into the stall and used toilet paper to wipe her panties. This had never happened to her before. She would have to ask someone why that had happened. Ila dropped the toilet paper into the toilet, flushed it and ran out of the stall to her class.

Ila ran into the class right when Mr. Dixon was calling her name. He looked up as Ila walked into the room. He announced her presence to the class" Well Miss Montgomery we are so glad you could join us." The class laughed and Ila went to her seat. She shared homeroom with Paula, and she could not wait to send Ila a note about Mickey. Ila got a tap on the shoulder and the girl behind her handed her the note. Ila opened the note and it read, "He is a bad boy." Ila turned and looked at Paula and she frowned. Ila turned back around and thought about the warmth in her panties and laughed.

The morning went fast with the changing of classes. Before Ila knew it, it was lunch time. Her gang had a favorite table and George the nerd of the group was always there first holding it down. George and Ila shared math classes together and she was beholden to him for letting her copy his answers on tests or spending time studying with her, math was her weakest class.

By the time Ila got to the table it was almost full. She sat at the end of the table. She opened her brown bag, P&J, chips wrapped in saran wrap, and four off brand cookies with cream in the middle. Ila always bought milk or soda with the lunch money she was given. Everyone's lunch was about the same, some had bologna, spam, egg salad sandwiches, chips, and off brand cookies from welfare. We never gave it a second thought. It was good and sometimes we had to share it with George because his family was considered poor. Little did we know we were all poor, but George's family was poorer. He did not have a father in the home. That is something that the rest of us knew nothing about.

Lunch was always fun, we all tried to talk at once. Sharon finally had a chance to scream across the table "So Ila what did Mickey have to say." Ila rolled her eyes at Sharon and said, "We can talk about it while we are walking home." Sharon rolled her eyes at Ila and started talking to Paula who was sitting next to her. The bell rang and they all disbursed to go to classes. Ila thought about Mickey all day. Ila had never cut class before; she did not know how to even do it. They called your house if you did not show up for roll call in your homeroom. What an experience that would be. Ila was daydreaming when George hit her arm because the teacher was calling on her. She decided to get that skipping school stuff out of her head.

The last bell rang, and everyone said good-bye to their teachers, and we all met on the corner to walk home together. Ila's Aunt Florence's house was on the street they walked on; she was going to stop by for a second to see if she needed anything. Aunt Florence had lost her legs to diabetes. Ila would go to her house at least once a week to clean the kitchen and mop the floor and run to the store if she needed it. After the tribe had gathered on the corner, we headed home. I let everyone know I was going to stop at Aunt Florence's house to see if she needed anything at the store. They walked the two blocks to her house. Aunt Florence was sitting on the porch. They all screamed, "Hi Aunt Florence." You could see her face light up. Ila opened the gate and ran up the steps. "Hi Aunt Florence, do you need anything from the store?" Ila said. Ila bent down to kiss her on the cheek. Her smile was still going from ear to ear. Aunt Florence responded, "No Ila, but can you come on Saturday and help me clean the house?" Ila responded "Sure, I will be here at 11:00 a.m." Her smile got even bigger. Ila kissed her again and ran down the steps to join the others. They all said together, "Goodbye Aunt Florence." And her smile came back instantly.

The group had walked about two additional blocks when Sharon decided it was time to talk about Mickey. "So, Ila, what did Mr. Mickey have to say to you this morning." Ila responded, "He just talked about himself, and we did not have much time to talk because I did not want to be late for homeroom roll call." Not wanting to leave it alone Sharon said, "Are you going to introduce him to your friends?" Ila replied, "I thought you knew him; you pointed him out at the basketball court." Sharon said, "I know of him and his reputation. He is my kind of guy." Ila laughed. "OK Sharon, if we see him again, I will be sure to introduce you." Then everyone else said, "What about us?" Ila laughed and said, "OK, I will introduce everyone, but we will probably not ever see him again."

The gang was dropping off as we walked home. Paula, Sharon,

and I walked up Mulford Street to our respective houses. I saw Mr. Burns sitting on the porch and I knew he was waiting for Sharon to check in at home, drop her schoolbooks and she would be on the porch touching his dick, he could not wait. His house had awnings in the front and on the side and was dark, it was hard to see what was going on even during the day. But what Ila did not understand was that his wife was in the house. Did she never come out to the porch to see what was going on?

Ila could hear the machines and opened her eyes to the bright lights of the emergency room. Her head felt like she had been hit with a hammer. There were tubes running up her nose, in her arms. Her wedding dress had been ripped in numerous places and there was blood everywhere. She began to thrash around in the bed, setting off all kinds of alarms. A nurse ran into the room and said, "Ms. Montgomery everything is alright, you are in the emergency room, and we are running tests and taking blood." You will be admitted for continued observation." Ila replied, "Is Brock here, where is he?" She started screaming his name "Brock, Brock, I am in this room, where are you? Brock, Brock." She saw another nurse enter the room and place a needle in her IV. Ila could feel her eyes slowly close. The nurse had sedated Ila because of her head injury and any quick movements could cause more harm.

The nurses looked at each other. It was going to be devastating to tell her that Brock was alive but if he survived, he would probably never walk again. One of the two bullets went straight through his stomach to his spinal cord and severed it. The other bullet was removed, but he had lost a lot of blood. It would be touch and go either way.

Ila ran into the house. She wanted to get her homework done so that she could go back outside. She ran upstairs to change her clothes to fold or hang them up because she may have to wear them again during the week. There was a wringer washer in the basement, but the clothes had to be hung out to dry. And sometimes the weather was less than cooperative, then the clothes had to hang in the basement. Ila's mother and grandmother really had a lot to do. She thought to herself when I grow up someone else will be doing my laundry. She changed clothes, made sure the room was straight and took her books from the bed and went downstairs to do her homework at the dining room table. It was kind of hard to do homework there because people were always coming in and out. But they respected the fact that she and her siblings had to do their homework, so they were as quiet as possible. It was also difficult because her mother or Grandmother were usually in the kitchen cooking and her stomach would start to growl. As that her was long gone. She often wondered why the school thought if you had lunch at 11:30 a.m. you would not be starving by the time you got home at 4:00 p.m. She completed everything but her math. She and George would do it together at lunch. Their math class was after lunch. She was so grateful to George. She would see if her grandmother would put extra cookies in her lunch so that he could have a couple. Or she would just give him hers. She finished history and English. She double checked her answers and decided that they were good. She closed both books and placed her books on the table in the hallway so that she could pick them up on her way out the door. She ran to the kitchen to see what was cooking. She spoke to her grandmother, and she wondered where her mother and Father were. Jack's car was outside. "Grandma, where is mom and dad." Ila said. Her Grandmother turned to her and said, "Elephant." That was her way of saying that it is none of your business. Her grandmother then said, "Dinner will be ready in an hour, and you better be close to the house or in whistle range." Ila laughed and said, "OK." She knew better than to be out of whistle range. She ran outside and the street was full. Hopscotch on the street, jacks on Paula's porch, the old men from the apartment building up the street were lined up to watch the young girls walk home from high school smoking weed and drinking mad dog 2020 or Iron City Beer. They were nice older guys, but Ila did not know why they called her Peaches. She would just scream at them, "My name is not Peaches" and they would burst out laughing. She decided to go visit her uncle who lived down the street. As she walked down the street, she looked over at Mr. Burn's porch and there was Sharon standing in front of him. Ila acted like she did not see her on the porch. She walked to her uncle's house and greeted him; he was drinking a root beer and smoking cigarettes. Her other Aunt was sitting on the porch next door, and she screamed at Ila to come to her house. "Yes Auntie," Ila said. Her Aunt gave her a piece of paper and a quarter. "Take this up to Mr. DeLeo at the store, he will know what to do and here is a nickel for you." For a nickel Ila would walk several blocks and Mr. DeLeo's store was right up the street. Her Aunt said that he would give me a piece of paper back and bring it right back to her. My Uncle screamed at my aunt, "Stop being lazy, sending her up to the store to play your numbers." Ila had no idea what that was, she just knew she had a nickel and tomorrow morning that meant at least one donut for her. She dreaded walking by the guys at the apartment building, but she knew what they were going to do, so she just laughed and walked past them and for sure "Hey Peaches," they all laughed, and Ila screamed "That is not my name" and everybody laughed. On the way back she would cross the street but that would not make any difference. As she got to the corner to cross the street to the store, she looked, and Mickey was standing outside of the store smoking a cigarette. Her stomach got tight. She looked both ways and crossed the street. She walked slower hoping he had not seen her, and he would walk away. No luck. He looked up and saw her walking down the street. When she got to the entrance of the store he said, "Fancy meeting you here." Ila smiled and said, "I have to go do business for my aunt." "Oh" he said, "Your Aunt plays the numbers too." Ila just looked at him. Playing the numbers was what everyone was talking about. She thought her aunt was paying off a bill. Mr. DeLeo would let the neighborhood come and get groceries and he kept a list of what it cost. When the men in the neighborhood got paid, you went into the store and paid your bill. She walked past him hoping that he would be gone by the time she was done. Ila walked in and saw Mr. DeLeo at the end of the counter waiting on another customer. She waited patiently.

When the other customer left, she walked up to Mr. DeLeo and gave him the note and the quarter from her aunt. "Hi there, Jack's daughter, what do you have for me?" He looked at the piece of paper, and then took a piece of paper by the cash register and wrote down .25 on #7. He handed the piece of paper to Ila and said, "Keep that in your pocket and give it to your Aunt right away and please tell her I said hello." Ila nodded her head and wondered why he smiled so wide thinking about her aunt. Then she thought her Aunt and Mr. DeLeo liked each other. She just shook her head and said to herself, that could not be possible. Mr. DeLeo was white. She headed for the door hoping that Mickey was gone. But then she saw his smoke rings in the air and knew he was standing to the side of the building. She thought when I get older, I am going to learn how to blow smoke rings. She again laughed to herself. "Hi again," Mickey said. Ila just looked at him. "Ila, I am going to walk you home." Mickey said. Ila's head turned around and she said to him "please don't, the entire block will know I was with you, and someone will tell my father. You do know you have a reputation." Ila replied. "Ok, so we will take the long way, we can walk to Tioga, and I will walk you through the alley and you can go to your house from the back way," he said. Ila said, "You know where I live?" Mickey just laughed and said, "Let's take the long way." I promise I will be a good guy." They headed down Brushton Avenue headed towards the alleyway. Ila did not give it a second thought that the Johnson Brothers may be in the garage.

They walked in silence for a few minutes. "Are you half Indian, because you look like you got Indian in you." Ila looked at him and did not respond. Ila looked at him and said, "You do know I am only 14 years old." Mickey responded, "I am only 18 years old, so what is your point." "So, you could go to jail trying to be with me." Mickey laughed," Who said I was trying to be with you." Ila's face got red. "I will not make you do anything you don't' want to do, I promise." "I think you are beautiful, and I just want to spend time with you until I get shipped off to the Army, is that a crime." Ila could feel her panties getting wet. Dang, what was going on. He reached out to hold her hand, Ila pulled back. As they walked, he talked about how he decided not to go back to school and how he had a rough life growing up in the Hill District. As they got closer to the Johnson Brothers garage, Ila was hoping that they had all gone home. Then she heard the voice "Ila, your Daddy know you walking the alleyway with boys." "Oh high Mr. Johnson, this is my brother's friend Mickey, Mickey this is Mr. Johnson." Mr. Johnson said, "I don't give a shit what his name is, does your father know you in the alley with boys." Ila replied, "No, Mr. Johnson." "Well, I suggest you take yourself through the alleyway to your house and you should do it now," he replied. Nice to meet you Son, but I don't want to see you with her again." Mickey was smart, he did not say a word except "Yes sir." Ila made a right and Mickey made a left but before he left, he said, "I will see you in the morning at school." Ila ran/walked to the alleyway that led back to her street. No one seemed to notice that she came from the alleyway except Sharon. Ila walked to her aunt's house, who had been drinking beer most of the day, so she had no idea how long Ila had been gone and her uncle had gone in the house. She walked up onto her aunt's porch and gave her the piece of paper. She thanked Ila and told Ila to say hello to her parents. Ila ran down the steps and started walking home.

Sharon had come off the porch and had money. "Ila, walk to the store with me so I can get soda, lunch meat and bread for lunch tomorrow." Sharon said. Ila knew that she had gotten money from Mr. Burns. Sharon usually had a span sandwich, raisins, and Cheetos. Sharon could not wait to get real lunch meat. If she was getting all those groceries, he must have given her two or three dollars. Ila did not say a word, she just fell in step with Sharon, and they walked in silence. There was nothing Ila could say about her friend playing with an old man's dick, but Sharon's family was poorer than everyone else on the street, so Ila understood. She had to wear the same clothes sometimes during the week and her saddle shoes were wearing out. They walked past the men at the apartment building, and nothing was said. Ila had never noticed that they had nothing to say when she was with Sharon. We got to the corner and Ila was praying that Mickey was gone. They looked both ways and there he was coming back down the street; he must have stopped at the bar. Ila again acted like she did not see him. "Hey Ila, hold up." He screamed. Sharon looked down the street and her face made a frown. Ila knew that Sharon liked Mickey and she could not believe that he wanted to spend time with Ila. Both stopped when they got across the street and waited for Mickey to meet them in front of the store. Mickey trotted to the front of the store and said, "How good it is to see you three times in one day." Sharon looked at Ila and looked at Mickey and stomped into the store. Ila told Sharon that she would wait for her outside. "You know Sharon likes you right." Ila said to Mickey. Mickey just shook his head and said, "Sharon is trouble, I only like girls that don't give you trouble" and he smiled at Ila. Ila was nervous standing out in front of the store with Mickey. There were eyes everywhere. Ila turned around so that her back was to the street. Mickey said, "You're scared to be seen with me." Ila did not reply. At that point, Mickey began rubbing the back of her neck and Ila's knees buckled. Mickey laughed out loud and started jogging down the street. He yelled back "See you in the morning." Suddenly Ila heard the whistle. And she heard the guys at the apartment building start screaming "Whistle." Ila ran into the store to see how much longer Sharon would be. She was headed for the door. When we got outside, Ila said, "My Dad whistled for me." They both started running. If Ila did not get home soon, she would be punished and what would Sharon do without Ila to hang around with. She was mad that Mickey liked her, but Ila was her best friend. As they passed the guys at the apartment, they all screamed "Whistle" and started laughing. Ila hit the steps as her father Jack was going into the house. He turned around and said, "You had about two more minutes." Ila ran up the steps and said goodbye to Sharon. Jack stood at the door and let Ila walk through. Everyone else was at the dinner table. Ila took her seat, Jack sat at the head of the table said grace and then all the tension went out of the room. Ila's mother looked at her and just smiled. Ila's mother understood her and her rebellious attitude. She never got to be rebellious. She got married early. Went from her parent's house to Ila's father's house. But when she looked at Jack there was a love that Ila wanted in her life, with her family when she got older. The table turned to chatter, and food was being passed, and Ila was happy to have a complete family.

Eugenia and Officer Waters sat straight up as both of their beepers went off. Eugenia had no idea where her beeper was. Officer Waters went straight to his uniform and looked at the text message 10-999, Officer down. He ran to his uniform and began getting dressed. They must have been calling him on the radio inside of his car. He had no intention of staying at Eugenia's this long. "Shit" he said out loud. Eugenia looked at him and knew that there was a real problem. She remembered that the beeper was in her purse, she ran over to all the items that were piled up from the wedding, found her purse and looked at her beeper the only words were Langley. She ran into the bathroom, splashed water on her face and was leaving the bathroom when Officer Waters headed for the door. "Come get the door and don't leave without your gun. I will call you later." Eugenia walked to the door and locked it as Officer Waters took the steps two at a time. She ran back to the bedroom, found her jeans, panties, bra and top and put them on quickly. She decided to wear the tennis shoes that Ila had brought them to wear after the wedding. Picked up her ankle gun, placed it on but left her other gun as she would have to surrender it at Langley anyway. Looking for keys, she remembered that her car was at Georgetown University and her keys were in Stephen's pocket. She went to the house phone and called a taxi. She then looked all over the house for cash. She came up with $100.00. She was sure the Taxi driver would not be making a scene once they got to their destination. She got her leather jacket, secured the apartment, grabbed her purse, and decided to wait on the steps for the cab. She thought she would be waiting forever. It was early New Year's day, but the taxi was there in approximately seven minutes. She heard the taxi coming down the driveway. The taxi was not even at the bottom of this driveway before Eugenia jumped into the back seat and told the Taxi to take her to Langley. The taxi driver looked at her and said, "Langley in Virginia?" Eugenia replied, "Yes Langley in Virginia." The taxi driver turned the car around immediately and headed to "G" street. He had never been to Langley but knew that the lady in the back seat had to be someone important. He headed to the George Washington Parkway. It was only about a 15-minute drive. His passenger had nothing to say. Eugenia sat in the back Thinking this must be about Ila's wedding. She had no idea what she was going to say to the agents who were going to interrogate her about what exactly happened.

Officer Waters raced down "G" street, the officer was down on Wheeler Street S.E. Those were the Green Valley projects, notorious for drug use and distribution. Officer Waters remembers when it was a place for families to grow and live peacefully. Then crack ravaged the neighborhood and the same families who had dreams of growing and moving out of the projects got stuck as family members became addicted to the chemically enhanced cocaine that was sold in the neighborhoods to stifle the growth and keep the residents in place, not to expand or spread their wings but to make sure that their reach was only as far as the five blocks of the projects. He knew it was done on purpose. Suddenly having crack cocaine in any weight was a felony and distribution could cause you to spend life in prison, but cocaine users were placed in addiction programs and given community service. Officer Waters knew the answer to the sentencing and treatment but could not think about crossing the blue line and voicing an opinion. He also knew that whatever tactical maneuver was being used in Green Valley by the police was like walking into the lion's den. The group of young men who ran the drugs in Green Valley may have been uneducated but very educated in tactical matters, especially tactically securing their neighborhood. They must have been shorthanded to put out an all-points bulletin, he could just turn around, he was a patrolman for PG County, this was way out of his jurisdiction, but the call came through they must need help securing the perimeter of the area. He sped through the streets with lights blazing to get there in the most efficient manner. He admitted to himself a long time ago that he really got a rush when the sirens were on and being a police officer was the only thing he ever dreamed of being. As he drew closer to Wheeler Street, he could see all the lights flashing. He saw other officers from Virginia and Maryland on the perimeter and decided to park on the perimeter to get the story on the officer down. He pulled along the sidewalk, made sure his weapons were secure, left the lights on, placed the patrol car in park and got out of the car. He walked to the other patrol car that was PG County to get the scoop on the situation. Officer Connors was standing next to his vehicle, weapon in hand. Officer Waters was just about to start asking questions when gun fire broke out. He saw Officer Connors fall to the ground and then he felt his kneecap collapse. The bullet shattered his kneecap, he could see the blood and white meat on the ground as he fell face first to the concrete. He fell next to Officer Connor whose chest was open with blood oozing out and he heard a final scream of pain and his eyes rolled up, his mouth wide open and blood running across his body. He screamed "Man down," officers were returning fire and he heard someone say, "Window." One of the Officers from Virginia returned fire to the figure in the window and then the world was silent again. Officer Waters was in so much pain, and he could feel his body becoming weak and saw the blood he was emitting. The only thing he could think of was that Eugenia was probably pregnant and he may never see his son or daughter and his wife would be a widow. That was his last thought, he did see the ambulance lights approaching and fell unconscious.

Eugenia thought the taxi would never get to Langley. As they approached the gate, she could see from the meter that she had enough money to pay for the taxi. When they got to the checkpoint, she showed the officer at the gate her ID. He told Eugenia to remove herself from the taxi and they would call for transportation inside the compound. Eugenia gave the taxi driver $60.00 and thanked him. The officer told the taxi driver to make a quick U-turn and to make sure he left the compound immediately. Eugenia exited the taxi and stood next to the police officer while she waited for transport. The officer then requested that Eugenia surrender any weapons she might have on her person. She reached for her .22 on her ankle and gave it to the guard. He placed it in a clear plastic bag and put her name on it. Within five minutes a golf cart approached the gate. The officer told Eugenia her transport had arrived. She walked through the gate that had a guard house and hopped on the golf cart. It was chilly outside; she felt the least they could have done was send a car. She sat back and could not believe the circumstances of the last 24 hours. She still did not know if Brock was dead or alive or if Ila was alright. She knew for certain that Stephen was dead, and Morris had escaped maybe. She was also truly uncertain about the gentleman who rescued her at the Church, and what was his name again? She shook her head and decided that all those things could wait because she was about to be placed in the Greek coliseum and questioned about what she did not know. Then she began to sweat. With all that had happened, she had totally forgotten about the two bodies that she and Stephen left at the Marriott in Crystal City. "Shit," she thought, I hope it is not about that. They were very thorough cleaning up and did not leave prints. She was sure it was not about that. It could only be about the wedding. The gentleman driving the cart did not introduce himself; he drove fast but professionally. Eugenia thought they would be going through the front entrance, but as they came upon the entrance, he turned to the back of the building to the other check point. He slowed up at the checkpoint, showed his credentials and went through the gate. Eugenia had not spent a lot of time at Langley, she had never even seen the building he was taking her to. Now she was really getting nervous. He stopped the car in front of a two-story building that looked like something out of a plantation slave movie. He creeped up to the front door and slowed down. Then he said "We have arrived at your destination, please go through the front door, and make a right, the conference room is the first room on the right. The Company will provide transportation back to your dwelling when the meeting is over." Eugenia thanked the gentleman who talked like Lurch from the "Adams Family." Eugenia grabbed her purse and walked slowly up the flight of stairs leading to the plantation house. She opened the door and closed it and then made a right to the conference room. All the lights were on, and she could hear voices in the distance. As she turned into the conference room, there was coffee, fruit, biscuits with different jellies and juice. Well, she thought maybe this is a friendly fire meeting. She looked around and slowly helped herself to coffee, fruit, biscuits, and jelly. She was hungry and she could feel a slight turning of her stomach. Dang, she kept forgetting she was pregnant. That was the most real thing about the last 24 hours, and it brought a smile to her face. After gathering up all her food, she grabbed a napkin and sugar and sat it in the middle of the table. She wondered when the meeting would start, she knew she was on camera, so hopefully they would wait until she got through eating. She unfolded the linen napkin and placed it across her lap and dove into the fresh fruit, strawberry, cantaloupe, grapes, and berries. She wanted to get up and get another plate but decided against it. She then ravished two biscuits with jelly and washed them down with cranberry juice. Sufficiently full, she got up, placed the dirty dishes back on the counter, poured another cup of coffee and returned to her seat. It seems as soon as she put her second cup of coffee down, in walked Mr. Snap and her stomach churned. So, this was going to be about the wedding. Well, all she could do was tell the truth, well most of it.

Ila finished dinner first, she jumped up from the table, took her plate to the kitchen, rinsed it in the sink along with her silverware, dried everything and put it away. This way if everyone washed their own dishes, the only thing you had to do was the pots and pans. It was not Ila's turn to do pots and pans, so after her dishes were washed, she stopped by the table and asked if she could go back outside till the streetlights came on. Her mother looked at Jack and he nodded his head. Ila's Mom said, "Do not leave the street." Ila smiled and ran out of the house. She said that like it was a punishment. There was so much to do and see on the block, you did not have to leave it to have fun. Ila sat on the porch feeling so secure, it did not matter where she went, there was family and friends. She could not imagine growing up anywhere else. Little did she know that within a year, they would be moving to the suburbs and her life would take an incredible turn. Sharon was walking up the street with a smile on her face. That could only mean one thing, she had money. She walked up the steps. "I got money," she said. "Let's go to the other store and get taffy apples." Ila shook her head, "Not allowed off the street Sharon." Sharon said, OK, I will take the short cut through the alley and come back with taffy apples. Ila looked at her and said, "You are going through the alley, it is getting late, I don't think that is a good idea." Sharon laughed and said, "You are such a scaredy cat," I will be right back. She ran across the street to the alley and disappeared. Sharon got halfway down the alley and started to walk and not run. As she got closer to the end of the alley, she could see a man standing almost at the end under a tree, as she got closer, she saw that it was Mickey. What was he doing in the alley? Then from behind the tree came a young lady, he handed her some money, and she walked out of the alley. Mickey looked up the alley and saw Sharon coming towards him. He waited because he knew she had the hots for him, and he had money, so he was going to make his move. She looked like an experienced young girl. Sharon began to walk a little faster because it was getting late. When she got to the tree where Mickey was standing, she acknowledged him. Mickey said, "Sharon, where are you going and why are you in the alley." Sharon stopped and looked at him and asked, "Why are you in the alley?." Mickey replied, "Taking care of business." Sharon responded, "I am going to the store to get Ila and I some snacks." "Oh," said Mickey," Would you like some more money for the store." Sharon looked at him and thought she could use some milk, bread, and chipped ham for lunches for the week. She replied, "Sure. Are you going to give me some money?" Mickey replied, "Nobody just gives you money, you have to work for it." Sharon looked at him as he rubbed his dick. She began walking again down the alley and Mickey screamed out, "I got $10 for you if you want to do a little work." Sharon stopped dead in her tracks so she could get taffy apples and then go to Mr. DeLeo's and get groceries for the week. She turned back around and walked to Mickey and said, "So what kind of work do I have to do and let me see the $10.00." Mickey took the

$10 out of his pocket, rubbed her neck, and slowly placed the $10 bill in her bra. "Here" he said, "Take the $10 and I will put you to work some other time." Sharon stood there with her mouth hung open. She had never been given this much money for doing nothing. Mickey said, "Go now, it is getting dark, I will hang on the corner until you leave the snack store. Are you going to Mr. DeLeo's afterwards?" Sharon replied "Yes." "OK," he said "Get going and we will see each other again." Sharon took off down the alley, crossed the street being careful on the streetcar tracks to the snack store, got taffy apples for she and Ila, came out across the street and headed to Mr. DeLeo's store. She was so happy; she would not have to struggle to eat lunch for the next week. She did not know what she was going to tell her mother, but she would probably be passed out on the couch anyway, so she would just place all the items in the refrigerator. She would be glad to see them when she woke up. She ran down the street to DeLeo's. She had to run because it would be closing any minute. She got to the door and Mr. DeLeo was headed to lock the door. He saw Sharon and waved for her to come in. Sharon ran to the cooler, got milk, went to the bread aisle and picked up white bread, ran to the next aisle and got peanut butter, jelly, and mayo. Ran to the next aisle, got sugar and Kool-Aid. She took all her things to the counter and waited for Mr. DeLeo to check her out. She looked at the lunch meat and wondered if she had enough money. Mr. DeLeo had gone to the front door and locked it because if neighbors saw the store was still open, they would still be coming in. Mr. DeLeo came behind the counter and began ringing up her items. She wanted to save some of the money but decided to ask him for ½ lb. of chipped ham. He looked at her and said, "Just ½ lb." Sharon replied "Yes." Mr. DeLeo left the cash register and moved over to the meat counter. Took the ham out of the cooler and placed it on a chipping device. The chipped ham would last so much longer. It was very quiet in the store, she was not used to not having other customers in the store, but she was not afraid of Mr. DeLeo, just felt a little strange. Mr. DeLeo, chipped almost a pound but only made Sharon pay for ½ lb. He rolled it up in white paper and placed a piece of masking tape on the package to keep it closed. He walked back over to the cash register and told Sharon that it would be five dollars and .50 cent. She pulled the $10 dollar bill out of her bra and handed it to Mr. DeLeo. He thought to himself, that is an unusual place for a young girl to pull her money from. He was used to it from the older women in the neighborhood but not the young girls. He unfolded the bill and placed it in the cash register. Sharon got her return change and was so happy. She placed the return change in the brown bag. She already had a bag with the taffy apples, so her hands were full, and she had no pockets. She thanked Mr. DeLeo and walked swiftly out of the store. As she walked through the store, she could see Mickey across the street. She waved at him, crossed the street and screamed out thank you once again. As she walked past the group of men who were sitting outside of the apartment building, they all started screaming, "Hey Sharon, what you got in the bag, can we have some." And they would burst out laughing. Sharon had no idea what was so funny, and they did not either because they were all high off weed, beer, or wine. Sharon just laughed out loud. She could not wait to leave this part of town, to live in Penn Hills or Squirrel Hill or Swissvale. She was going to make enough money one day to move out of this neighborhood. Ila was still sitting on the porch waiting for Sharon. She was starting to get worried as the streetlights came on. She heard the men laughing loud and knew that Sharon was on her way down the street, and she did not come through the alley. Sharon stopped at the hedge at Ila's house, pulled out her taffy apple and Ila jumped off the porch to get it. She looked at all the groceries Sharon had but did not say a word. She thanked Sharon for the taffy apple and Sharon continued down the street. Ila jumped back on the porch and began the process of eating the taffy apple. You had to bite it just right on the side and work your way around to the end and then go for the top. Suddenly she heard the screen door slam and out came her father in crisp pants and a light blue shirt and his Sunday shoes, he had his famous hat in his hand and Ila could hear her mother screaming, "You better be back before you go to work at 11:00 p.m. Jack did not say a word, stepped past Ila and said, "I'll be back." Jumped in his beige Chrysler and took off down the street. She knew her mother was probably in the house crying so she decided to stay on the porch until her grandmother told her it was time to go in. It was going to be a long night.

The bodies that had arrived at Walter Reed Hospital over the New Year's Eve weekend were incredible. Dr. Gregory White had just finished his residency and was now a full-time doctor at Walter Reed. It started around 7:00 p.m. on New Year's Eve and bodies came flying in the emergency. One man DOA, the other with bullet wounds in the stomach, and a woman with head injuries and a police officer whose neck had been 8slashed. He had been pronounced dead at the scene. The DOA had keys to a car which he gave to the secret service when they arrived. The body was also transferred to the morgue in a special holding. The man and woman were sent to a special guarded wing of the hospital. He had no idea who these people were or who they worked for, but he knew that special treatment had gone into effect as soon as they reached the hospital. The police officer's body was sent straight to the morgue. And, he just got a call from emergency that several injured were coming from a shootout in Southeast Washington. There are days he really thought this was not the right move to make with his life, but then the people that you save out ways the stress of the people you lose all worth it. He ran to the elevator, headed down to emergency and as he turned the corner, he could see all the blue and red lights flashing and bodies being taken out of ambulances from many districts. It was going to be a long night. As he headed towards the emergency triage, he heard the head nurse call out rooms, "This one to room 4, This one to room 7, This one to room 6, and all hands were on deck that were not being utilized in other areas of the hospital now. He ran into the area and went to room 7, to see what he could do for that patient. A nurse and PA were already in the room. The nurse was cutting off the uniform and the PA was securing the police officers firearms in a bag and the doctor could see the bottom of his leg dangling from the knee cap. The right leg was all but gone from the kneecap down. His badge said his name was Officer Franklin Waters. They did not want an infection to set in, so they rushed the Officer to surgery. Orthopedics was not his specialty; they would have to call in a specialist for this operation. The nurse called George Washington University to see if their lead orthopedic/prosthetist doctor could come to do the surgery. The scheduling head nurse at George Washington University said that he had just come out of surgery. The nurse explained that it was a police officer that had been attacked in southeast Washington and was in danger of losing his leg. The head scheduling nurse replied he will be there in 30 minutes. Dr. White decided to concentrate on the other officers that had other injuries not as severe as the Officer with the severed leg. He went to room 4 to assist only to see that the Officer was dead on arrival. He left room 4 and went to room 7 and they had the officer stabilized and was ready for surgery. He somehow was also hit in the knee, but the bullet must not have had a direct impact, it might have ricocheted off something during the gun battle. He went to the sink, threw away his old mask and got a new mask and headed to surgery to see if he could assist with stabilizing the officer whose leg was severed. Upon entrance to the operating room, he placed operating gear on, placed shoe covering on his feet and entered the operating room. The blood had clotted at the knee but the rest of the leg was still hanging on. They had managed to close the other wounds that must have occurred during the fall, and they had the patient heavily sedated. The head nurse came in minutes later and announced that the orthopedic doctor was in the building and would be in surgery shortly. The team made small talk and the surgical nurse prepared the room for the orthopedic doctor. The room fell quiet as the doctor entered the room. The doctor read the chart quickly, assessed the situation, checked for a pulse close to the cut, removed the diseased tissue and any crushed bone and smoothed out uneven areas of the bone. He sealed off as many blood vessels and nerves and began cutting the leg off with a Gigli saw and like a plastic surgeon skillfully rounded the stump so that a prosthesis could be used in the future. Dr. White was in awe of this doctor. He had a skill that was masterful. The police officer was very blessed to have a doctor of this caliper work on his leg. At the end of the surgery, the surgical team began clapping their hands and the team looking on behind protective glass also clapped their hands. The doctor never said a word. He walked towards the door, removed all his surgical clothes, and left. Dr. White soon followed to complete his shift. He had been assigned to the police protected ward for the night. He was going to go to the staff cafeteria, get a cup of tea and a small sandwich and begin to make his rounds. His first patient was Ila Montgomery. He wondered what her story was and how she ended up in a protective ward on New Year's Eve.

Ila sat at the window waiting to see if her father would come home before he was supposed to go to work. She fell asleep in the window seat. When she woke up it was 1:00 a.m. and her father's car was not parked out front. Her only hope was that he had come home before going to work, changed his clothes, kissed her mother deeply and went to work. She crawled into bed next to her sister. It seemed that she had just laid her head down when she heard her mother screaming, "Ila get up," everyone else is up and getting ready for school, you know I must go to work." Ila sat up slowly. Dang, she hated being the last one to use the bathroom. Most of the hot water had been used, her brother always used her toothbrush because he did not care whose toothbrush he used. Ila finally got smart and began taking her toothbrush to her bedroom and placing it in a plastic cup. She grabbed her toothbrush and ran down the hall to the bathroom. Her mother heard her footsteps and decided that screaming one more time would not help. - Ila's grandmother always made her lunch, so all her mother had to do was place it on the dining room table and she would pick it up while picking up her books. Lorraine had four children, the first three at a very young age. She will never experience the things that her children will experience in the world, but she was alright with that. Her other children had already left for school and her youngest was sitting on the porch waiting for her to take him to daycare on the way to work. He had to go to daycare three days a week as Grandma went by bus to Squirrel Hill to clean the Orthodox Churches three days a week. Ila screamed down the steps, "Ma, don't forget my milk money." Lorraine went into her purse and left a dollar by the lunch bag. She screamed up the steps, "I left you a dollar which should last the rest of the week. Don't ask me for any more money this week." "OK," Ila replied, "See you after school." Lorraine went to the back door to make sure it was secure and to see if the dog was chained to the poll. All secure. She never worried about Ila locking up the house, she was a scary child, so she did not want anyone to come into the house. Lorraine laughed out loud and went through the three doors necessary to get into the house. She hopped into the Chrysler as she had missed the carpool and got mad as she could smell the residue of beer and perfume in the car. Her youngest son just rolled down the windows and said, "Mommy it smells in here." Lorraine did not reply.

Jack had come home before he went to work but he smelled like a distillery. He took a quick bath, changed into his uniform, grabbed her, and kissed her deeply and went to work. Lorraine was very tired, as soon as the house was secure, she went to bed, the next thing she heard was him coming back in the door at 7:20 a.m., taking off all his clothes and falling into bed and began snoring loudly. She laughed to herself. He thought he was such a player, but truly his playing days were slowly coming to an end. Her youngest son kept him busy with baseball, football, hunting, soccer, and any other sport he could come up with. Activities that they could not afford with the other children when they were young, but they all knew how to swim, read a map, take care of dogs, study hard and keep part time jobs while in school. There was not much more she could ask for. She was sure that her oldest daughter would go to college. Her oldest son was skilled in many areas; he just had to choose his path. And, Ila, she just shook her head, then there was Ila. She laughed again, turned over the car and pulled out to start her day.

Ila had not taken the time to clean off her oxford shoes the night before, so she took a minute to wipe them off with the cloth used to clean the bathtub. Which needed to be cleaned. She was sure it was her turn to clean the bathroom. She would do it as soon as she got home from school. She wore a red pencil skirt and a white blouse, white socks, and her shoes. She had a small makeup bag that her mother had given her for pencils, pens, and erasers. Her mother even left red lipstick, a makeup sponge and half a mirror in the bag. The first time Ila opened the bag at the beginning of the school year she could not believe her mother had left her lipstick. Inside the bag was a note that read, "I know you are wearing lipstick so here is a good tube so you can stop sneaking around." Ila laughed but she knew that lipstick better be off by the time she got home. If her father saw it, all hell would break loose. He told her she had to be sixteen before she could wear lipstick. Right, all the girls were wearing lipstick and she was too. She placed Vaseline on her lips first, ankles, elbows, and face. Then she put on her lipstick. She could hear her friends screaming her name from outside. She ran downstairs, grabbed her lunch and the dollar bill. Placed the dollar bill in her bag, turned off the light, locked door one, locked door two and left the screen door unlocked. Paula and Sharon screamed, "You are going to make us late." Ila laughed because they always said that. Of course, they walked quickly to DeLeo's store to get three glazed donuts. They were a nickel a piece. Sharon of course had money and a large lunch bag. Ila just laughed. Paula had money, so they were all good to go. Getting their donuts, they headed towards Hamilton Avenue to pick up the rest of the gang on the way to school. It was September and the air was getting chilly. In Pittsburgh it is cold from Mid-

September until May of each year. Ila could not wait to move out of Pittsburgh. She did not like the cold and dreamed of living on a tropical island.

They all walked and talked. It seemed that the 15 blocks took no time. As they got closer to the school, Ila looked up on her aunt's porch to see if she was sitting out. But no one was on the porch. She would be back down on Saturday to help Aunt Florence clean the house and go to the store. It was Thursday and they all could not wait for Friday because there was a party in Belmar Gardens that they all were looking forward to going to. Sharon's friend's parents were going out of town to Harrisburg and her friend was throwing a party while they were gone. Ila could not wait; she had a red jumpsuit that her mother had found at the five and dime store and she had not worn it. As they entered the gate, who was standing about five feet away, Mickey. Sharon looked at me and said, "There is your boyfriend." Then I heard his voice "Ila, Ila, let me holla at you a minute." The gang all said together "Ila, let me holla at you a minute" and they all burst out laughing. Ila was pretty sure he was not allowed on school property if he was not a student, but he seemed to get away with it. She walked down the sidewalk to greet him. "Hi," she said. "Hey, he said, how about you go to your homeroom, get checked in tomorrow, and I will meet you at the side door on Hermitage Street." Ila looked at him. She had never skipped school before. He said "I will borrow my friend's car and we will go to Frick Park and have a picnic. No one will see you there. I will go to the corner store, get hotdogs, chips, and pop and then we can walk to the bottom of Frick Park and have a picnic on a sheet." Ila looked up at his green eyes. She could smell the cologne old spice on his skin and the raw scent of cigarette smoke on his clothes. She could not wait to learn how to smoke. She kept looking at him and did not say a word. Finally, he said, "You are going to be late for homeroom, I will see you tomorrow at 8:40 a.m. at the side door." He turned around and walked away and left Ila standing there like a mannequin in a store window. She snapped out of it, turned, and ran to the opening in the front gate, ran up the steps and ran to her home room. Once again, the teacher was just calling her name. "Ila, you are cutting it close these days." Ila walked fast to her seat and felt the warm sensation in her panties and started to blush. She looked up at Paula who started to laugh in her arms. They both did.

Sharon could not believe he called Ila's name and not hers. They were just in the alley together. He gave her money. If he thought he could play both, he was wrong. She was going to tell Ila about how she met him in the alley and how he gave her money. Then Ila would not like him anymore and he could become her boyfriend. She would tell her on the way home. But when the school bell rang for the end of the day, Sharon remembered that Ila and Paula had chorus after school. She walked home with the rest of the crew noting to herself to tell Ila tonight or first thing in the morning.

Mr. Snap sat down in a chair directly across from Eugenia. "Hello," Mr. Snap said "My name is Carlton Watson, and I am the lead investigator for the Marriott Hotel murders of two

Company men in Crystal City. Would you know anything about those murders?" Eugenia wanted to sit straight up in her chair, but she knew that was a sign of defiance, so she stayed in her comfortable position with her legs crossed and replied, "No sir, I don't, and it is very nice to meet you Mr. Watson." "The name of one of the men was Maurice, he was an operative. Did you know him?" "Oh my God Maurice is dead. That is tragic, what happened." "It looked like a gangland style slaying, but it was too sophisticated, it seems they were killed, placed in a bathtub and a solution was poured on their bodies to help with the decomposition. We are not sure of the solution that was used." Eugenia did not reply. "We are waiting to get information from the hotel surveillance camera for that time to see if we can recognize anyone coming and going during that time. What is funny Ms. Eugenia, we found a cassette tape and player that came back with your fingerprints, so how do you believe that player got into the hotel room with your fingerprints on it." Eugenia was silent for some time. She did not want to respond incorrectly. "Mr. Watson, it was rumored that Maurice was staying at Ila's old apartment, he could have taken it to the hotel room and of course my fingerprints could have been on it as I have been on Ila Montgomery detail going into the second year. There is no telling how many fingerprints I could have left on items that belonged to Ila. But again, I cannot help you." "Well, we will wait for the hotel camera footage, I hope to not see you in any of those frames. Will I see you on any of the cameras, Eugenia?" "I am sure you will find who killed those gentlemen, you seem like a very accomplished investigator. If I hear anything in the underground,

I will certainly let you know." At that moment a uniformed officer came into the room and whispered into his ear and left. Carlton stood up and said, "Several police officers from different precincts have been shot in Southeast in a shootout with drug dealers, we have an operative inside the drug gang we need to get him out quickly. This is not our last conversation. Eugenia we will speak again. A driver will be here within minutes to take you back to your apartment. Oh, by the way congratulations on being pregnant, I am sure that circumstance will have your desk bound somewhere in the very near future. That way we will be sure to be able to find you. Be prepared to turn in all your credentials, welcome back to civilian life." With that he left the room. Eugenia was stunned and a tear rolled slowly down her face. She knew there were no secrets in the Company, but she really thought this secret she could have kept a little while longer. She thought it was against the law for doctors to talk about their patients' medical condition. Oh, that's right in civilian life, but not with the Company. Then she began to laugh and cry hysterically. What if Officer Waters was involved in the shootout, he left the house in a hurry. There is no way she was going to raise a baby by herself. He better not have been involved in the shooting; he better not leave her baby fatherless." She sat in the chair and used napkins to wipe her face. "Pull yourself together," she said in her head. She had no idea where all that emotion came from and then suddenly, she was hungry again. She went back over to the serving table and got more breakfast food. She knew the cameras were on her and would be used against her later if they found more evidence. She never gave the cassette player another thought and neither did Stephen. They were so careful. That is why they say there is no such thing as the perfect murder. Well Stephen was dead and dead men tell no tales and she was a lifetime operative, there is no way she was going to confess to being involved with that situation. They better find some additional evidence, or she was walking away clean. She started to laugh, they already knew that Maurice and Hunter were HIV positive. They both went to Walter Reed hospital. This murder will be claimed as a murder suicide between lovers. Paperwork will be placed in legal size brown folders and marked, Company confidential and placed in a safe somewhere in Langley. She had been around too long not to know how the story was going to end. As she sat and ate, she could hear people arriving to start their day at work. It did not matter that it was New Year's Day, the Company was open essentially twenty-four hours. She wondered where the driver was, and as soon as that thought crossed her mind there, he was standing at the door. "Excuse me Miss, I am here to take you to your designated location." Eugenia wiped her mouth checked for her keys and walked towards the door. "Designated location," now she wondered if she was going to make it back to her apartment. She would be sure to send a 911 message on her beeper to Franklin as soon as they were on the road. Most communication devices were blocked at Langley unless they were on the network. As they drove through the gates, they stopped so that Eugenia could retrieve her gun then, he made a left towards DC. She could feel her heartbeat slow down, but she still was very uncomfortable about where this man was taking her. She finally asked him, "Do you need to know the address of my designated location?" He replied, that won't be necessary, I have the address in Georgetown. She could feel the air leave her body. Maybe not this time, but there will always be a next time. The only reason she is still alive is because of the baby. This situation would be cleaner if everyone involved was dead. Thank God for life.

Officer Franklin Waters was placed in a private hospital room with a guard. His wife Joyce had been by his side ever since the surgery ended. She knew this would change everything in their lives. Franklin was not a man who was going to easily accept being without a leg. Franklin had also lost two fingers on his right hand as it seems when the officer next to him got shot, he caught his hand also. Joyce had wanted her marriage to have a new beginning but not this way. She knew he had been seeing other women, but she felt he would soon retire from the police force, and they would be able to rekindle their love by spending more time together. This meant spending more time together in an entirely different hemisphere. She would be taking care of him. She knew that the distance between them was not all his fault. As she too had been having affairs, one that had been going on for a year. She looked at her husband and hot tears rolled down her face. What would be next? This was a path she did not expect.

Paula and Ila decided to walk home. They could have taken the activity bus that was provided for students that had extracurricular activities. Plus, Ila wanted to tell Paula that she was cutting class tomorrow to be with Mickey. Paula was very quiet and smart. She did not talk to many people. She was light skinned with freckles and her dad had red hair. They were a different family. Her Dad worked as the Fuller Brush man and her mother was a homemaker. Some of the women would sit on the porch and talk about her mother being able to stay home. Ila felt they were a little jealous. But Ila knew that Paula's mom had a nervous condition, so she could not work. Paula would cry because her mother would not come inside in the evening, all she wanted to do was sweep the porch and the steps. And her father came home late every night. "Paula," Ila said, "I am going to cut class tomorrow and hang out with Mickey." Paula did not say a word. They walked along a couple of blocks when Paula said, "Can I come." Ila stopped walking and looked at Paula. "You want to come. Are you sure, you are a straight A student and I know you have never missed a day of school? We both could get into big trouble if we got caught. Paula screamed "I don't care, I want to come, please take me with you." "Ok, OK, Ila screamed back, but this is our secret, you cannot tell anyone including Sharon she would flip like a jack's ball if she knew we were cutting school with Mickey." "I promise," Paula screamed and started laughing "I can't wait." Ila began to laugh too; she was a good friend." They started walking faster to get home knowing that the next day was going to be a great adventure. Ila dropped Paula off at the end of the street as she got closer to her house, she saw Sharon on Mr. Burns' porch. You would think she would get tired of pulling on that old man's dick. But she liked the money, so she pulled whenever she could. Ila walked silently in front of the house. She could hear Mr. Burns tell Sharon, "There is your little friend, why don't you ask her to join us sometime." Then I heard Mr. Burns yell. Sharon must have pulled hard on his dick. Ila started laughing and ran the rest of the way home.

Jack's house was a buzz. Tomorrow was Friday and Ila's parents were hosting a quarter party for a neighbor who could not pay their rent. Most people gave a dollar at the door, so Ila was always curious as to why they called it a quarter party. Nevertheless, everyone will have a great time. Grandma was in the kitchen cooking and Ila's mother was in the dining room setting up for the next night. Everyone would have to eat at the small kitchen table tonight. Ila's mother Lorraine was putting the top on the dining room table and placing card tables up in the living room. People who did not want to play cards would go into the basement and smoke weed and listen to the music on the victrola in the basement and shoot dice. The basement had a separate entrance that Jack would monitor. He was not a card player, but he loved to smoke weed and throw dice. Most of the money from the party would come from the basement. What ended up happening is that most of the women would be upstairs and the men would be downstairs. They could only have the parties during the spring/summer months because the winters in Pittsburgh began around mid-September and did not end until April. Ila knew she would not be staying in Pittsburgh; she disliked the snow and wintery cold months. Ila dropped her schoolbooks in her room, changed her clothes and began cleaning the bathroom as she knew that sooner or later her mother would require it to be cleaned. It was not that large, so it did not take a lot of time. She began with the tub and wiped down the shower curtain, took all the towels and placed them outside the door. Her Grandmother would wash them on Friday morning. She placed her father's and mother's items in a small cabinet underneath the sink. She went to the linen closet and got more bathroom tissue and paper towel and placed it on the back of the toilet. Everyone knew that after tonight, to take their towels to their respective rooms and not leave creams, lotions, etc. in the bathroom because those visiting the party would use them. Each of the bedrooms had locks on the doors, so all the bedroom doors would be locked until the party was over usually around 11:00 p.m. on the first floor and the guys would go until two a.m. in the basement and they would just go pee in the yard or in a bottle. Ila decided to just clean the floor on her hands and knees with a bucket of water and ammonia. She did not feel like going downstairs for the mop, etc. Once finished, she left the bucket in front of the bathroom, so everyone knew they had to take off their shoes to use the bathroom until the floor was dry. Ila loved her bedroom; it had a large window that looked onto the street, and it had a window seat. She could sit there and watch as life on the street went by. She also saw things in the bushes in the alley that most young girls should not have witnessed, but she could never take her eyes off the things that happened in those bushes. She sat in the window seat and fell asleep. She woke up when her sister walked into the room and began changing her clothes from school and she heard her mother calling for her up the steps. She knew her sister wanted time alone, so she left the room and went to the bathroom to pour the water down the toilet that was left in the bucket and place it under the sink and hang the washcloth on the "U" pipe under the sink. She took the towels from the second floor to the basement to be washed. Her mother was standing in the kitchen by this time. Her grandmother had finished cooking and was sitting at the kitchen table. "Ila," her mother said. "Did you do your homework or were you sitting in the window and fell asleep." Ila's grandmother just laughed "You know what that child was doing." Ila did not say a word, she just continued to the basement. There was a coal furnace in the basement. The coal company delivered coal and we had to feed it in the winter like a fire breathing dragon. The heat that came out of the radiators was intense. She left the towels in the wringer washing machine. She looked around the basement and realized how fortunate they were to have heat and to have a family. Her brother would use his BB gun to shoot mice and rats during the winter when they came in to get out of the cold. This was also something that she knew was not going to be in her future house. Ila would live in a warm state, it would not have a basement; it would have many levels up, but no basement. She could not wait to see that house. She would draw the house and landscape and it always had hills behind the house. One day, one day. "Ila Maria what are you doing in that basement, get up here and wash your hands for dinner" her mother yelled. Ila loved Friday night party nights because she could eat in the backyard on a small table on the porch and have her dog eat anything she did not like. When they were inside her parents watched her like a hawk because she generally hated all the vegetables her mother and grandmother loved, brussel sprouts, cauliflower, and okra. But today they were having meatloaf, mashed potatoes, and green beans, one of her favorite meals, so she was more than willing to be first to eat. She laughed as she took the steps up to the kitchen two at a time. Both thanked her for cleaning the bathroom without being told. Her mother handed her a plate of food, a fork, and a glass of red *Kool-Aid*. Starving, Ila wasted no time eating her food. Victor would be very disappointed tonight as she loved everything on her plate, but she would share some of the meatloaf because her mother had given her so much. She could hear her brother and sister enter the kitchen to get their plates and they would go to their respective places. Her sister went to their room, her brother to the front porch to sit on the swing. That was usually dedicated for grandma, but she had eaten and was now sitting in the living room watching the black and white television set catching the evening news with Walter Cronkite. Ila's baby brother spent most of his time with grandma so wherever her grandmother went, so did her little brother. Ila finished her meal, took her dishes into the kitchen, washed them, and put them in the drainer. She did not believe it was her turn to clean the kitchen, but she would not get out of the house without someone yelling out, "It's your turn to do the dishes." She walked swiftly from the kitchen to the living room and told her grandmother she was going outside; she had no idea where everyone else had gone. She knew this was the time that her parents spent together in the bedroom as it was really the only time for intimacy. Ila laughed at the thought of her parents doing the "Nasty." Ila stepped onto the porch and her brother, and his two very handsome friends were on the porch. Ila was only allowed to acknowledge them. Anytime her brother thought that one of them was paying her too much attention, he would get mad and send everyone home. She waved and began walking down the street when she heard Paula's voice behind her. She waited for her to walk down the street, Paula had taffy apples in her hand, she was hoping that one of them was for her. Paula walked up and gave Ila a taffy apple and they both sat on the curb to enjoy the delicacy. Paula said, "So what are you wearing tomorrow?" Ila looked at Paula like why does it matter what we wear. "I saw Mickey at the corner store, we should walk up there and tell him I am coming with you, so it won't be a surprise," Ila looked at Paula and said, "You want to cut school more than I do." They both laughed and finished their treats. You could not hold a conversation and enjoy the taffy apple, so they sat in silence and watched people come and go. They looked up and Sharon was coming out of the alley. She looked a little crazy, her hair was messed up and her knees were dirty. Paula looked at Ila and they both laughed. Sharon yelled" What are you laughing at." Paula said, "Well your hair is a mess, and your knees are dirty, and what were you doing in the alley?" Sharon looked down at her knees and spit in her hand to wash them off, we laughed again. Sharon took her hand and tried to knock her hair down. Ila and Paula laughed even louder. Then the boys on the porch started to laugh. Sharon was so mad she ran down the street to her house. Paula and Ila laughed until tears were streaming down their faces. What had she been doing in the alley? Ila and Paula walked over to the water hose that was on the side of the house, turned it on, drank from it and washed their hands and faces from the sticky taffy apple. "Come on" Paula said. "Come on where" Ila replied Paula rolled her eyes at Ila, "let's go talk to Mickey." Ila rolled her eyes at Paula. She had never seen this side of her. She wondered if she liked Mickey also. He was not all that, dang. "OK, OK, let's go see if he is still there. They walked up the street and stayed on the right-hand side so they would not have to cross in front of all the men at the apartment building. It did not matter they called out to us anyway, "Peaches and Yellow where you'll be going." Paula and Ila ignored them. If you said anything they just had more to say. They reached the corner and looked across the street, but Mickey was no longer there. They turned left to walk to the other store and there he was standing by a tree near the alleyway. It never dawned on either one of them that Mickey and Sharon had just had an intimate session in the alley. They both walked up to Mickey, he started smiling from ear to ear. "Well to what do I owe this pleasure." Ila looked at Paula and then looked at Mickey and said, "Paula wants to cut school with us tomorrow." Mickey did not say anything for a few minutes. He looked at Ila and said "Anything for you. I will tell my cousin to come with us. He does not work Friday and Saturday." This is really going to be a real party. Well now Paula welcome to the party. This is going to be a lot of fun." Paula's face turned beet red. Ila started laughing because it had just gotten real. "See both of you at 8:40 a.m. tomorrow at the side door," Mickey said. Ila looked at Paula, her face was finally going back to normal. They both said goodnight to Mickey and turned left again to walk up the alley before it got too late. Mickey walked behind us to make sure we got through the alley unharmed. He did not walk to the end because he knew there were people on the street that would see him.

It was beginning to get dark, so Paula and Ila parted ways. Paula was grinning so hard Ila thought her face would crack. Ila laughed, ran up the stairs and went into the house. She could not contain herself. She went straight to her room to finish her homework. The house was beginning to settle down. Ila thought it was wise to get her bath in early as others would be coming to use the bathroom. She ran down the hall and started her bathwater and screamed downstairs, "Anyone got to go to the bathroom, come now." There was a toilet in the basement, but only the boys used that toilet. She waited about five minutes. When no one came, she went into the bathroom and locked the door. You were not supposed to fill the tub up, because it cost too much money. But Ila took the liberty to put just a little more water in the tub that night. She wanted to make sure everything was clean. She used her sister's hair removal to take away the hair under her arms. There was too much hair on her legs to worry about, she just let that go. She washed every part twice and she knew her time was up. Someone would want to use the bathroom very soon. She slowly got up out of the tub and pulled the chain plug. She hated using bath towels more than twice. She vowed that when she got older, she would use a new bath towel every day. She dried off and placed her nightgown on and placed her sister's hair removal in the exact spot she left it, or all hell would break loose if she thought Ila had used it. She poured the cleanser in the tub and then went through the back breaking job to clean the claw foot tub. It was so deep. But if you did not clean it and well, there would be screaming all over the house, like someone had died. Ila laughed out loud. What a crazy family she had. Ila was going to go downstairs and put the hot comb on her hair but decided just to put some gel on her hair and place it in curlers. She hoped that her edges were not too nappy in the morning. After cleaning the tub and the floor with a sponge, Ila went back to her room to hang the towel and washcloth on the steam radiator to dry the towel. Ila looked under the bed in her secret shoe box to make sure the make-up she had purchased was still there. She was going to take the little pouch with her in the morning so that she could put on lipstick and mascara after getting to school. She would wear a skirt with pockets. She ran to the closet to make sure that one of the two skirts that had pockets was clean. She found her blue skirt and a light blue thin sweater that would look nice. The light blue thin sweater was her sister's, but she went to school first, so she would not know she had it on. She found clean white socks and took her towel and wiped off her saddle shoes. She had a clean bra and her Friday underwear.

Morning came quickly. Ila moved slowly as usual so that it did not look like she was doing anything different. But Paula was at the door 20 minutes early. Ila's Mom had not even left to go to work yet. She could hear her mother's voice talking to Paula in the hallway asking her why she was so early, and that Ila was still getting dressed upstairs. Thank God, Paula was quick on her feet, no wonder she was a straight A student. I could hear her telling my mother that she was hungry and that her mother had not gotten out of bed to fix any breakfast. Of course, then I heard my grandmother yell, "Come on in, baby, there is bacon and toast in the kitchen." Her mother side-eyed Paula as she ran into the kitchen to be with Ila's Grandmother. Ila was not about to come downstairs until her mother was gone. She had a way of looking at Ila and knowing that she was up to something. Ila walked about her bedroom for about 10 minutes waiting for her mother to leave. Her brother and sister had already gone, and her younger brother was sitting on the porch. She heard her mother leave. She grabbed her books, placed the package with her make-up in her skirt pocket, checked her hair and walked swiftly down the hallway to the stairs. She wanted to take the steps two at a time but decided against it. At the landing of the steps, she turned into the dining room and walked into the kitchen where Paula and her grandmother were sitting. Her grandmother was sitting there having hot water with lemon and Ila would not know until many years later why she did that every morning. Paula looked up from her bacon and toast and smiled. Ila sat down and got bacon and toast from the large plate in the middle of the table. "Good morning grandma." Ila said. "Morning Maria." Her grandmother replied. "Where is your jacket? I think it is going to get chilly this afternoon." Her grandmother said. "I will get one on the way out the door grandma." Ila replied. Her grandmother looked at her Timex watch and said, "Hurry now, you are going to be late for school." Ila quickly ate the bacon and wrapped her toast in a napkin. Paula thanked her grandmother and they both walked quickly out of the door. When they got to the porch, Sharon was walking up the street. Paula and Ila met her in front of the house, and they headed to the corner store to get donuts. They all knew Sharon had money from yesterday. They all looked at each other and laughed. After getting donuts they headed for school. Picking up classmates along the way and laughing and making fun of each other. The walk to school seemed to take forever. Ila's palms were sweating. Paula had very little to say on the walk to school. Sharon did most of the talking. She had been asked to go to the junior dance. Ila and Paula knew that they could not even think about going to the junior prom. They were not even really supposed to date unless it was with a group. She wanted us to go shopping with her on Saturday to find a dress. We all agreed that we would go with her. She was so excited. Ila promised to do her hair and makeup and Paula had great fashion sense, so she would help with accessories. Sharon must have been putting her cash away. She might have made money in a way that we did not appreciate, but she always had money. Unlike us, we had to make do on one dollar a week for lunch money. Most of us got free lunch, so the dollar was for milk, water, or soda. Finally at the gate of the school, everyone went in separate directions. Ila went directly to the bathroom to put on her makeup. Sharon went to the back of the school to do whatever before class and Paula went straight to homeroom. Ila finished her makeup in about 10 minutes and walked through the homeroom door just as the bell rang. Ila and Paula sat through the pledge of allegiance, roll call, and morning announcements. Finally, the bell rang. Ila and Paula met in the hallway. The plan was to go to the football locker room and go out the side door. Usually there was no one in the locker room during first period. They walked slowly greeting other students and hoping not to run into either of their first period teachers. Once out of the main hallway, they ran down to the basement, went through the double doors, and exited out of the boy's locker room. Ila and Paula never thought about people looking out the windows. They just wanted to meet up with Mickey and Sugarbear quickly. Mickey was standing outside of his cousin's car. It was a gray and black two door Riviera. They had no idea how old Sugarbear was, and Paula did not seem to care. Mickey was smiling from ear to ear. He folded back the car seat and told Ila to get in the back. He hopped in the back with Ila and Paula jumped into the front seat. Mickey did the introduction from the back seat. Sugarbear reached over and touched Paula on the hand. Ila could not see her face, but the side of her face began to turn red. Before they pulled off, Sugarbear placed a tape in his eight trac. Isaac Hayes Hot Butter Soul began to play, and they drove straight to Homewood Park. Sugarbear parked the car and pulled out a joint. Ila had smoked before with her brother and his friends, but she was sure Paula had never smoked. Mickey pulled out a joint for the two of us, and we all sat and smoked, listening to music. Paula was choking at first, but after a couple of puffs, she started to get the hang of it. Mickey and Ila talked about how he was going to enter the Service and how he could not wait to get out of Homewood. He had been there all his life, and most of the time it was a life that he could forget about. His father was incarcerated for theft, driving under a suspended license, and resisting arrest. Since it was not his first offense, they threw the book at him, and he was doing 10-15 years. Ila thought to herself, that was a lot of time for those charges, but little did she know that during that period in history, Black men were arrested for walking while Black. He talked about his half brothers and sisters and other members of his extended family. Ila was so surprised he was sharing so much information. Ila tried hard not to listen to the conversation that was going on in the front seat, but she looked up and Paula was undoing her ponytail. Sugarbear had convinced her to show him how long her hair really was. Shortly after the ponytail fell apart, Sugarbear started up the car, turned up the music and headed towards Wilkinsburg. Mickey had moved closer to Ila, and Paula had moved closer to Sugarbear in the car. Ila whispered to Mickey, "You did tell Sugarbear that Paula was a virgin." Mickey nodded his head and said "Yes, I told him we would be traveling with jailbait. He understands he can only go so far. We are just going to go back to his place to eat some grub, smoke some more weed and relax. Sugarbear stopped by Bethesda Methodist Church to see if they were cooking on the Church property. And of course, it was Friday, so the smoker, grill and fryer were in full effect. He pulled into the yard. He asked everyone what they wanted. It was unanimous, Fish and Fries. He jumped out the car, placed the order and walked back to the car and lit up the remainder of the joint and passed it to Paula. Ila and Mickey had smoked their entire joint, so Mickey lit a fresh one and they sat in the back and watched the clouds of smoke swirl around their heads. This joint was a little different, if it went to Ila's head fast. Ila said to Mickey, "This one is different, it is going straight to my head." Mickey responded, "Yes, I got this from my friend who grows it in his basement, he calls it black gold. I had to pay extra for it, but for you it was worth the additional money." He tapped Paula on the shoulder so she could try it. She coughed several times but kept pulling on the joint. Mickey started laughing hard, as she kept pulling on the joint. He finally pulled it from her hand. Paula was high but was enjoying freedom. Something that she had never had before. Sugarbear saw the man coming towards the car with the food and jumped out to meet him halfway. The man told him the cost and he pulled the money from his pocket and told the young man to keep the change. Sugarbear jumped back in the car, placed the food between he and Paula, started the car and turned up the music. By this time, they were feeling no pain. They all began to sing to Isaac Hayes. Sugarbear headed up Homewood Avenue. Paula turned and looked at me, we were very close to home. Then he took a quick right onto Bennett and a left into the alleyway. Sugarbear lived in the row houses off Bennett. It was a nice family community. During the overheard conversation, Sugarbear told Paula he worked for a hospital as a patient coordinator. He wanted to be a nurse in the diabetic ward. His mother died of a diabetic complication. He was starting community college in three or four months. He pulled in the back of a row house with a chain link fence. Sugarbear lived on the first floor, and it had its own entrance from the alley. They all jumped out of the car and manually locked the doors. Paula had gotten comfortable. She grabbed Sugarbear's hand as they walked up the sidewalk to the door of his apartment. Ila rolled her eyes in her head; this chick was really gone. But she was enjoying herself. They entered the apartment to a large living area, which had a couch, three bean bags, a TV, and a coffee table. There was a small kitchen off to the right of the living room. They all went to the living room and found places to sit. Sugarbear had a boombox on the floor, he walked over and turned it on to the local radio station. He gave everyone a box with their meal in it. Paula and Ila wanted to wash their hands, so they walked to the bathroom together which was off to the left of the living room next to the bedroom. Ila wanted to talk to Paula a minute before the rest of the day took care of itself. They crowded into the small bathroom. "Paula are you OK?" Ila asked. "Yes, never felt better, I really like smoking." Paula said and began to laugh. "Paula, please make sure Sugarbear knows you are a virgin, this is not the day you have to give up your cookie." Paula looked at Ila and said, "Speak for yourself, I am giving up this cookie today. I am tired of being a virgin, it is time I lived my life." Ila knew that was the weed talking. "Paula, wait and see if you like this guy, plus he is 21 years old he could get in trouble dealing with you." "Only you know Ila" Paula looked me in the eye, let me enjoy this day without thinking about my family situation, without me having to think about the fact that my mother is crazy, and my dad is never home and runs the street with other women. Just once Ila, let me not think about how I may never go to college because I may have to take care of my mother? Ila threw up her hands and said "Paula, you are my best friend, please be careful." Paula flipped her hair and said, "You be careful, I am going to have fun." Ila looked at her and laughed out loud. Who was this person? They both laughed and washed their hands.

Mickey spread his food and Ila's food out on the coffee table. "Sugarbear, you know that girl is a virgin, don't do anything with her. She has no idea what that would be like." Mickey said. "Man, you should not have brought that sweet yellow thing into my web, she is going to get got today but I will be gentle." Mickey looked at him and said, "You may be opening a can of worms, you might not want to." Sugar replied, I will just put the worms on a hook and go fishing." They both laughed, but Mickey thought to himself, he hoped this fool knew what he was doing, this one day could ruin his future. Ila and Paula exited the bathroom and Ila took a seat next to Mickey on the couch and Sugarbear took Paula's hand and headed towards the bedroom. Paula turned swiftly to follow him into the bedroom. Ila heard the music turn on in the bedroom. Sugar came out of the bedroom and went to the kitchen to retrieve beer for he and Paula and told Mickey to help himself. He walked past them, went into the bedroom and closed the door.

Mickey got up and went to the kitchen to get beers for him and Ila. The beer was nice and cold. He was hungry, so he opened the beers and brought them back into the living room and placed them on the coffee table. Ila was waiting for him to return before she began to eat. She also wanted ketchup. Before Mickey sat down, she asked him to see if there was any ketchup in the kitchen. He placed the beers on the coffee table and went to look for ketchup. It was in the refrigerator. As he walked back, he turned it upside down as it was almost at the end. He sat down and pulled the coffee table closer to the couch. Ila was starving. She held his hand to say grace and he looked at her like" Why you are holding my hand I am ready to eat." Ila said a brief grace and Mickey smiled; he could not remember the last time he prayed over his food. They talked, ate, laughed and drank beer. Once the meal was completed, Mickey cleared the table and tossed the remnants of a good fish sandwich meal into the garbage can in the kitchen. He came back into the room, sat on the couch and pulled Ila's legs off the ground onto his lap and took off her saddle shoes. She had made it clear that she did not want to have sex and all he said was that he was going to give her a different experience. She was up for a different experience. He placed her shoes on the floor and then placed his hand on her thigh. He began rubbing between her legs. Ila could feel the warm sensation coming from her pussy and wanted to tell her brain to stop having those sensations. He worked his way up to her Friday panties and slid them down to her ankles and took them off and gently laid them at the other end of the couch. He stood up quickly and went to the bathroom and came out with Vaseline and a towel. Ila thought this was a good time to ask for another joint. She did and he went into his pants pocket, pulled out his last joint and lit it with a lighter that was on the coffee table. He laid Ila back on the couch and handed her the joint. She smoked it and closed her eyes as he took his fingers and opened her pussy moving slowly feeling her wetness, his dick began to grow. He stood up and took off his tennis shoes and his pants. Ila opened her eyes to see him in white briefs and his dick was sticking out like a tree limb. She closed her eyes again and continued to smoke the joint.

Mickey got up and went back into the kitchen to get an ashtray. He placed the ashtray on the table, took the joint from Ila's hand and grabbed her hand to stand her up. He took off her skirt, folded it and placed it at the bottom of the couch. He took the towel from the bathroom and placed it on the couch. He told Ila to get on the couch on her knees. She had no idea what that was about, but between the beer and the weed it sounded like the perfect thing to do. She laughed and jumped on the couch and got on her knees. Mickey took off his briefs and placed them at the end of the couch. He laid on his back and told Ila to sit on his face. Ila looked confused. Sit on your face for what she thought. This guy is crazy. She leaned forward and let her legs lay flat while using her elbows for balance. Mickey opened her pussy with his fingers and stuck his tongue into the lips of and flickered his tongue. Ila felt something like pee come from her vagina. It scared her. She looked down at him and he was really enjoying the flavors coming from her body, then her knees started shaking and her nipples became hard and tender. She could feel a scream coming on when Mickey said, "Let me know how you feel." Ila screamed with pleasure and began moving her hips up and down his face. He held on to her ass and dug into her vagina with force. Ila was cumming and screaming and screaming and cumming. Mickey began to laugh. Ila was embarrassed. He lifted her pussy off his face. Ila was laid out like a dishrag on the couch. Mickey let her sit for a minute and then asked her to turn around to place her head towards the back of the couch and get on her knees. Her pussy was still very wet, she was enjoying this new experience. Mickey parted her butt cheeks and began to lick the crack of her ass. She was so glad she had taken a bath the night before. She started to laugh to herself but then there was another new sensation, he had taken the Vaseline and placed it in her asshole. He took his thumb and pushed it in and out of her ass. It hurt initially then a pain that hit the top of her head started and went straight to her knees. He had taken the head of his penis and stuck it into her ass. He gently took the head in and out. Biting her ass and holding on to her breast with one hand. He was gentle and took his time opening her anus. Ila could not believe that this could give her so much pleasure. Then he said Ila , hold on. He slowly placed his entire penis in her ass, wrapped his arms around her waist and lifted her into the air slightly while pumping slowly at first and then more and more, harder, and harder, then Ila heard an animal scream like a deer had been shot come out of Mickey's mouth. He pulled her ass closer and closer; she thought his dick would come out of her mouth. She loved this feeling and did not want it to stop, but after the scream she could feel his hardness get softer and softer. He pulled out, grabbed the towel, and wiped her ass and her pussy, turned her around and laid her on the couch. He left and went into the bathroom. Ila heard the water running. He was cleaning off his penis. He came back out with the other end of the towel wet and cleaned Ila up. Took her panties from the end of the couch and placed them back on her. Ila had tears coming out of her eyes. She did not know what she was going to do with this feeling as she already wanted it to happen again. Mickey got dressed and handed Ila the rest of her clothing to get dressed. They looked at each other and Mickey said "That was wonderful. I hope you enjoyed that experience." Ila replied, "You have no idea." And they both laughed hard. Mickey took the remnants of the joint from the ashtray and lit it for them to finish. They both heard the bedroom door open. Paula and Sugarbear walked out of the bedroom hand in hand. Paula had redone her ponytail. Ila thought she should go to the bathroom and see what her hair looked like. Paula sat by Mickey and took the joint from his hand. Ila headed to the bathroom. She had to pee anyway. Once in the bathroom, she looked in the mirror and knew that this was a turning point in her life and things would never be the same. She saw a brush on the back of the toilet. She used it to smooth down her hair, went to the bathroom and joined everyone else in the living room. Mickey looked at the kitchen clock and said, we better roll. It is three o'clock. School lets out at 3:30 p.m., we will just make it back. They all picked up beer bottles and cleaned up some. They walked towards the door and Mickey pulled Ila back into the living room and kissed her hard. Her knees went limp again. Dang it, why did he have to do that. Then he said, "You cannot continue to miss school, so we will find another way to see each other." With that he took Ila's hand and walked her out the door making sure it was locked. Paula and Sugabear were already in the car. Mickey and Ila jumped in the back seat, and they drove back to the end of Monticello Street and dropped the girls off. They all said goodbye and the guys drove away. Paula looked at Ila and said, "You alright, do you want to talk about what happened." Paula replied, "Not now, but I am not mad we skipped school." They both laughed so hard tears were coming out of their eyes.

Then they both looked at each other, they had left their books in the car. Shit! She hoped Mickey would bring them to the corner store when he realized they were in the car. Just then they looked up and the car was coming back. Mickey jumped out and gave them their books and got back in the car and they drove away.

Eugenia had sent a 911 digital on her beeper to Officer Waters, but he had not beeped her back. The driver slowly drove down the driveway. Eugenia had a flashback of New Year's Eve. So much had happened in 24 hours. Eugenia was very surprised to see her car parked in the back of the apartment. Then she shook her head, that was not a surprise. Now she wondered where the keys were as Stephen had the keys to the car in his pocket as he hit the floor in the chapel. She thanked the driver as she got out of the car. The driver said, "I will be back on Friday to show you to your new location." He backed up the car and drove slowly back up the driveway. Eugenia stood there thinking Friday, how could a decision to move her have been made so quickly. Even after all these years, she was still surprised at how swiftly the Company could cover up and reinvent someone's life. She climbed the stairs slowly and suddenly her body felt like it had been hit by a truck. She placed the key in the lock and turned it and looked into a completely packed apartment. She turned and locked the door and walked through her apartment and saw that only the essential items were left unpacked. They must have had a crew of twenty people to be able to pack a complete apartment in four hours. Eugenia walked to the living room and turned on the TV and there on the coffee table were the keys to her car. She could not help the hot tears that streamed down her face. Stephen was dead, she had no idea about the conditions of Ila and Brock. Had Morris gotten out of the chapel safely, where was Officer Waters and where the hell was Paula. She was going to have a hot cup of tea, take off her shoes, when the house phone rang. Good afternoon the voice on the other end of the phone said, please retrieve the envelope left at your door. The line went dead. Eugenia walked to the front door and decided to get on her hands and knees and crawl to the door and open it slowly. She did not have her gun on her ankle as she could not take it into Langley. She crawled to the door and forgot she had placed the dead bolt on as she entered the apartment a few minutes ago. She decided if they wanted her dead, she would have been dead a long time ago. She stood up, unlocked the door and there it was the vanilla envelope. She reached down and grabbed the envelope and shut the door quickly and locked it. She could feel a twinge in her stomach. She was going into her third month, and it was incredible to feel movement in her stomach. She could not wait to be a mother; it was something that she never thought would happen. Then she heard a news bulletin, she ran to the TV and the announcements were being made about a murderous New Years weekend, with confirmed deaths and injuries from two separate incidents "A murderous shootout at the Chapel on the campus of Georgetown University and a police shootout in S.E., with officers injured and one dead. The name of the officer who died at the scene's name is being withheld pending the notification of family. The murders at Georgetown University are still under investigation. More details will be reported as these cases unfold."

Jerome and Anthony had just driven up the alley when a black sedan drove up to Eugenia and Ila's apartments. The driver got out of the car and left an envelope at Eugenia's door.

Eugenia stared at the television set and tears began to roll down her face. Her baby's father had been shot and was in critical condition and she did not know what to do. How was she going to find out how he was? Her partner in crime had just been shot to death, Ila was still in the hospital, Brock was questionable. She suddenly felt so alone. Exhausted from the two days of complete turmoil, she sat on the couch slowly laid down and fell into a deep sleep leaving the envelope on the coffee table.

Eugenia slept for hours. When she woke up it was dark, and the temperature had dropped, and the apartment was extremely cold. She decided to make a cup of tea. She was hoping that they had left out at least one cup and the tea kettle. She walked into the kitchen to find everything was still in tack. They were probably going to come back and pack the kitchen after she moved to her new location. She opened the refrigerator only to find it filled with fruits and vegetables. A pot of vegetable soup and honey baked rolls. On the side shelf there were vitamins, A, B, C, K, and iron. She started to cry. This was their way of telling her she was grounded from covert activity until the baby was born. Suddenly, she was not hungry, just tired. She closed the refrigerator door and slowly walked to the bedroom. They had left the bed made, but all her clothes were packed, and her guns had been placed in a case and left on the nightstand. It was cold in the apartment, so she walked to the thermostat and turned it to heat. It would not take long for the apartment to get toasty. She walked back to the door, made sure it was locked and contemplated turning on the front door lights. She decided to leave them off. She walked slowly back to the bedroom, removed all her clothes, and climbed into bed. The next thing she knew, it was morning.

Jerome and Anthony sat outside in the alleyway devising a plan on how to get into the apartment and to get Eugenia into their confidence. Tomorrow Jerome would place a call to Judge Randolph Pennington to make sure his cover paperwork had been completed and that his new name, Ancil Jerome Rogers, had a social security card, birth certificate, school records, etc., as the first thing Eugenia and her boyfriend would do is a background check. He and Anthony sat in the car for about 45 minutes longer. It was getting colder, and they had to run the car all the time. The smoke coming out of the exhaust will soon cause nosy people to call the cops. They drove off slowly and headed to Anthony's apartment. He was still enrolled in the University, but school did not start back until January 10, so he had a few more days off to help his father devise a plan to destroy Eugenia's life. She would pay for all those years he spent in prison. Anthony's apartment was not far from Eugenia's apartment. The brownstones were older and filled with students. Anthony had lucked out to get a basement studio. There were two studio apartments. The other apartment was a student who lived out of State and was gone a lot. Anthony was so glad he did not have to explain to anyone as to why his father was living with him. When asked, he told them that his mother had passed, and his father was living with him until he was able to find another place. Most fell for that story and did not come back with more questions because he would tell them his mother died. When in fact, she was in SE somewhere with some man still on drugs. She used to be beautiful, but crack use had taken most of her teeth and she was very thin. His father could not stand to look at her. But Anthony would go see her periodically and give her food, money, and clothing. He would never let his father know he was going to visit her for fear he would bust a gasket. They drove around the block three times hoping to find a parking space. Third time around someone was pulling out two doors down from his apartment. He placed the blinkers on and waited for the car to pull out of the space. His father was very quiet. He knew that the next five months were going to change his life. But he would do anything for his father. While he was in prison, he made sure that his aunt took good care of him. Made sure he had the best of almost everything including tutors. Anthony always struggled with science and of course he could not get into Georgetown with struggling grades and a low SAT score. But his father made sure that he had tutors, and he never received lower than a "B." He also paid for him to go to Catholic school, which Anthony hated, but in hindsight, it kept him on the straight and narrow and now he was going to Georgetown. He had to learn to parallel park living in Georgetown and had gotten very good at it. Once parked he looked over at his father and he had fallen asleep, something that he did not do much of and he had terrible nightmares. Once parked, he knew better than to touch his father. So, he decided to just get out of the car and slam the door, which would wake him up and sure enough it did. His father's eyes popped open. He looked around slowly, saw me standing outside of the car and was satisfied it was safe. He slowly reached for the car handle, opened the door and sat for a minute before getting out of the car. Looking up and down the street first. He looked up at Anthony and said, "We should walk to the corner for Chinese food. I am starving." Anthony nodded his head and waited for him to get completely out of the car and manually locked the door. They walked to the takeout in silence. He knew that his father would have a plan in the morning. They got to the walk up and ordered, it was cold outside so they decided to go inside and sit in the back of the small restaurant so his father could see the front door and Anthony could see the back door. Jerome knew they were going to move Eugenia now that all that went down at Georgetown. How was he going to make sure he knew what her next move was going to be? He had to call the Judge first thing in the morning to make sure all loose ends with his new identity were taken care of.

Paula and Ila turned the corner to begin the walk home. Ila saw Sharon and the others on the corner looking for them. Sharon spotted us first. She screamed "Hurry up." Ila looked at Paula and they began to run a little bit. When they caught up with everyone of course Sharon had something to say. "What are you guys doing coming from that end of the school." Ila chimed in, "We went to go look at the football players as they were practicing. You know I am in love with the senior quarterback Richard Johnson." Everyone started to laugh, and Sharon sang out "You are a freshman, he does not even know you are alive." Everyone laughed. Ila just started walking fast making them think that she was mad. Paula tried to keep up with Ila, but she was moving fast. When Ila got to her aunt's house, she told everyone that she and Paula were going to help Ila's Aunt with some chores around the house. She told them that they would see them later. Sharon looked very suspicious. Paula and Ila walked up the long steps and let the group go on up the street. Ila's Aunt was on the porch as usual. Aunt Florence began to laugh. "What do I owe this pleasure? " she said to Ila and Paula. "Hey Aunt Florence, we are just going to take out the trash and sweep up the kitchen floor quick. I will be back tomorrow afternoon to help more." Aunt Florence replied, "Great, but that is really all I need, my daughter came by two days ago and did most of the cleaning, but I do need the trash put out and the floor in the kitchen swept. You know, I try my best to get everything off the floor, but with both legs gone at this point, it is very hard." Ila and Paula nodded their heads and headed into the house. And there he was, Uncle Frank sleeping on the couch snoring as usual, sleeping off his drunk from last night or the night before. Ila did not understand how she could be married to a man like Uncle Frank but one day she told Ila "He was the most charming man she had ever met, and I love him." Ila decided that there was no talking about Uncle Frank, that was a fight she would not win. She and Paula headed to the kitchen. Paula went upstairs and emptied all the trash cans into one bag. She had a couple of replacement brown bags, so she folded down the ends and put them in the containers. She was coming back down the steps when she saw Uncle Frank coming up the steps. She froze. She had never seen him awake. She slowly walked down the steps. He never even acknowledged her. He passed her on the steps like she was not there. Paula was so glad. She did not know what to say to this grown man who smelled like alcohol, Old Spice and Murray's hair dressing. After he passed her, she ran down the steps. She ran into the kitchen where Ila had gotten the mop and placed bleach in the bucket after sweeping the floor. She could not find a dustpan, so she used an album cover. Paula looked like she had seen a ghost. "What's wrong," Ila said. "I just passed your uncle on the stairs, and he never said a word." Ila laughed, "he is probably still drunk. I have known him all my life and he still never really speaks to me unless Aunt Florence makes him. It is not a problem really. He won't remember you were even in the house." They both laughed. Paula took all the trash to the alley and Ila finished the kitchen floor. They sat on the back porch and talked while the floor dried. Paula started to cry. Ila was not sure what to say and then Paula said, "He was so nice. I told him I was a virgin, and he was so calm about it, and he took his time. He put Vaseline everywhere and he ate my kitty cat." "Your kitty cat, what the hell is that.?" Ila laughed hard. "You mean your pussy"? "Yes Ila, you are the only one who says that word." Ila thought about that and said, "You know you are right." They both laughed loudly. "Did he hurt you?" Ila said. "Yes, at first but it did not take long to feel good. I bled a little bit. But he had towels, I think he was ready." They both laughed. Paula said, "What about you?" "Well, he put his dick in my butt." At first, I was disappointed, but he told me he did not want me to get pregnant and that he would wait until I was old enough to get birth control before he would put his dick in my pussy." Paula looked at Ila. "He did use a condom right." Paula looked at Ila with tears in her eyes and said "No." Ila did not respond. She would have a talk with Mickey. How could his cousin have unprotected sex with a virgin? Ila looked at Paula and said. "Well, we better get going before we both get in trouble for coming home late from school." They put the broom and mop away. Poured the water from the bucket down the kitchen sink and placed the bucket in the closet. Ila locked the back screen door and inner door, as she knew that her aunt was just going to get a bite to eat and then go to the living room where she lived her life and watched TV. They walked silently to the front door. Aunt Florence was falling asleep. Ila touched her on her shoulder. "Hey Aunt Florence, we are all done." She looked up at us with her steel gray eyes and smiled. "Thanks baby, I am about to go in the house now. You two be careful walking home." She reached behind into the bag sitting next to her and pulled out two large peppermint sticks. Now you know she is a diabetic and should not have candy, but we were glad to see the candy. She gave us both a stick. We thanked her. As we reached the bottom step. She shouted. "Maria, you know I did not give you that." Ila laughed and shouted back "No we got them at the store." When Ila heard her call her Maria, she knew that it would be a secret between the two of them. They had a wonderful relationship. She just wished she knew her before she had lost her legs.

Paula and Ila walked in silence as they ate the peppermint

sticks like they were steak. They were both very hungry and hoped that whatever their families were having for dinner would be good. Paula might end up at Ila's house because her mother may not have cooked. They walked quickly. They would tell their parents they stopped at Aunt Florence's house. They would not be mad; just mad we did not tell them.

As Sharon walked with the group she looked back as Paula and Ila walked up the steps to Ila's Aunt's house and thought to herself. Something was going on with those two and she was going to find out what it was.

Ila dropped Paula off, but before she could get home, she heard Paula running behind her. "Ila wait!" Ila stopped and looked at Paula. She had tears in her eyes. I knew her mom had not cooked. Ila grabbed her hand, and they both started to laugh when Ila whispered in her ear. "Dick in my butt." Everyone was on the street. Sharon was on Mr. Burns' porch because his check had come in, so she was going to get paid. Paula and Ila laughed again. Ila's grandmother was walking toward the door. Her younger brother was walking up the steps and slowly the kids started to disappear. It was dinner time on the block. Ila and Paula ran up the steps and into the house. Went straight to the bathroom to wash their hands. Left the bathroom, went to the dining room, and started putting plates on the table. Ila's father Jack wanted everyone at the table for dinner. And that night he wanted dinner over so that the party could get started around 8:00 p.m. No one ever said anything about Paula being at the table all the time. It was no secret in the neighborhood. Actually, no one ever said anything when another child showed up at the table. It just meant that my mother and grandmother would have to be more creative tomorrow to make sure there was food on the table the next day. Of course, as a young teenager, Ila never gave that a thought, because she knew somehow there would be food. Everyone talked about their day. Ila's father Jack complained about President LBJ, and still talked about the death of John F. Kennedy. Ila's grandmother would talk about cleaning houses in the Jewish community and Ila's mother never had a lot to say, she listened a lot. The family dynamic was a little crazy. Ila had an uncle that was younger than she was. That was a story that the family never really talked about. Ila just left that alone. They all ate, laughed, fed the dogs from the table, cleaned up, swept the floor and went back outside. Homework would wait until Sunday.

Ila and Paula ran outside. They knew that it would be dark soon and they would be confined to the porch. They both ran down the steps and they heard Sharon's voice. "Hey, you guys look at what I got. Taffy apples for us all." Paula and Ila laughed. Sharon had gotten paid. The three of them sat on the curb and ate the delicious apples with sticky fingers. They would go over to the spigot on the side of the house and wash their hands after they had eaten the apples to the core. They had just washed their hands and were about to walk to the corner store to spend more of Sharon's money when they all saw Mickey at the same time. He looked so good. He had on a patchwork sweater, black pants, and a pair of black and white Chuck Taylor tennis shoes. He walked over to the three girls and said, 'hello ladies, I wish you were old enough to go out, I would take you all with me." They all laughed, and he crossed the street and walked towards the alley. When they could no longer see him, Sharon shouted, "I really like him. I want to be his girlfriend. Hey, I will see you guys later." She proceeded to walk to the alley. Ila and Paula stood there in disbelief. Tears streamed down Ila's face. Paula could do nothing but rub her back.

Eugenia woke up. She felt terrible. She sat on the side of the bed and felt irritation in her stomach. It felt like she had to throw up, but she choked down the feeling. She put her pants and the top back on and slid into her slippers. The problem was she had not eaten, and the baby had to be fed. She could feel that the air had changed, and it was cooler today than yesterday. She walked to the kitchen and looked for crackers and found some in the cabinet. Every time they refurbished the food, they moved things around. She stood over the sink and ate about ten crackers to settle her stomach and placed water in a cup from the kitchen sink. She then walked over to the refrigerator, and pulled out berries, cantaloupe, cheese, hummus, and thinly sliced salami. Now, if she were not pregnant, she would never eat salami, but on this day, she spread out that meal like it was the last supper. She got a plate and ate in silence. It was 10:00 a.m. and she was eating like it was lunch time. As she ate, she reviewed the last two days and could not believe how her life had changed. She got up and placed water on the stove for tea. It was a gas stove so it would not take long for the water to boil. She sat, ate, and listened to the silence of her apartment. With the kitchen on the back side of the apartment, it was hard to hear the hustle and bustle of the busy street outside the apartment. She had not heard the whistle from the tea kettle as she had drifted off to a place where no lady is supposed to go. She turned off the kettle and looked for where they might have placed the tea, she opened every cabinet and finally in the last cabinet she found tea bags of green tea, all the rest had been taken away. She had not done any research, but someone had. She figured if she had to drink tea the company coordinators found out this was the tea she could drink. She wanted to get an update on Franklin but was really scared to even turn on the TV. Then she remembers the envelope. Eugenia walks back to the living room and retrieves the envelope from the table and walks back to the kitchen to finish her tea. Eugenia slowly opened the envelope and there were keys with tags. Apartment keys, new code for beeper, new bank and insurance cards and a new ID. Her new name was now Margaret Patterson. The handwritten note read as follows:

- Your belongings will be moved on Friday at noon, be prepared to follow the movers to your new location.

- New apartment is completely furnished.

- Please use your new ID immediately

- Your new domicile will be located on Glebe Road, close to the Ballston Metro stop and the Arlington Hospital where you are registered to have your natal appointments and to deliver your child.

- Bank accounts have been changed.

- Insurance cards, changed.

- All payroll payments will be paid directly to the new accounts.

- You will not receive a new assignment until your pregnancy commences.

Any questions, call the Company.

She left the envelope on the table, walked back to the bedroom, and got back in bed. She had no idea that being pregnant would also mean being horny for nine months all the time. Her toys were all packed up, so she took the time to think about the last time she and Officer Waters were together and slowly placed her fingers on her clit and rubbed slowly, then faster, and within 10 minutes, she had completely exploded in her hand. She wiped her hand on the sheet and fell fast asleep.

Jerome laid awake on the pull out couch his son had in his apartment. He could hear his son's snoring through the walls, not crazy but loud enough to disturb his sleep. He should be used to it by now. All his cell mates snored, but he would hit the outdoors as soon as he was able and worked out in the yard. He had privileges, so he got to go out to the yard with about ten other guys early in the morning before the general population was allowed to go. He started his own vegetable garden and had work duty three times a week in the kitchen. It was hard to get communication out to his colleagues and family, but then one day in walked Judge Randolph Pennington. His other roommate had been released and he was waiting for his new roommate to arrive. The guards had told him that he was getting a special roommate, one that had had sex with a minor, but by the time the trial came around the young man was now 20 years of age, and even though the sexual act was consensual, the young man was still a minor at the time of the act. Their relationship went on until he was 19 years of age and then they were caught in the parking lot of the courthouse. The Judge was having his dick sucked and a security guard walked up to the car and saw the act. Fast forward, the Judge got 5 years in prison but did not have to register as a sex offender and could practice law after the five years, but it could not be in family court, only criminal court and not cases involving sex with minors. The criminal system at its best. Jerome had all the information on the Judge, his wife's name, his children's names, where they went to school, etc. He would not let the Judge know how much he knew until an appropriate or necessary time. He walked in nervously. Jerome reached out and shook his hand and welcomed him to paradise. Jerome had managed to get many books from friends and family. He told the Judge to help himself to anything he wanted to read. He also told the Judge that if he knew of anyone that could send more books to him that it would help him to make friends. The Judge nodded his head and walked slowly to the bunk on the right side of the room. Jerome had taken the bunk beds apart. He did not want any roommate of his to get a jump on him by being in the top bunk. This way he slept with one eye open and could be cognizant of every move his roommate was making.

The Judge laid his belongings across the bed and Jerome was

surprised to see a device that looked like a telephone and a briefcase. He did not say anything, but Jerome understood that if this was a telephone, he was going to be able to communicate to the outside world from now on. His heart started beating fast. There is so much he could do if he had the ability to talk to the outside world. He was going to play it very cool to make sure that he found out exactly what was in that briefcase. He made the Judge feel comfortable asking him if he wanted a little jailhouse wine. The Judge laughed and said "Yes, at this point I will need whatever you have just to get to sleep tonight." Jerome took the paper cups he had stored away out and poured the Judge a cup of wine out of the bottle that the guards' thought was a power drink. He handed the cup to the Judge and returned to the book that he was reading. It was probably a book that he should not have been reading considering it made him mad at every page. But it was well written, and Jerome wanted to keep his reading skills up.

Jerome shook his head back to earth. The only thing he wanted to plan and or think about was making that call in the morning to the Judge to find out where they were moving Eugenia. He slowly let his mind relax so that he could get some sleep. A good night's sleep was out of the question, he had not had a good night sleep in 20 years.

Jerome woke up to the noise of the street. He slowly rolled out of bed and walked to the window to check the weather. It did not look like snow or rain, but it was cold. Jerome had not been able to join a gym but did go to the gym with his son on the campus of Georgetown. He could still hear his son's heavy breathing coming from the bedroom. He walked to the kitchen and grabbed a glass and went to the sink to get a glass of water. DC had the worst tasting water. He let the water run for a while to get what he thought were the chemicals out of the pipes first. He drank the entire glass. Most people take getting a glass of water from the sink for granted, but after being incarcerated for so long, everyday things were a luxury. He placed the glass on the sink and walked over to his suitcases. He had been living out of his suitcases since September. The Judge of course did not have to do his five years. If Jerome was not mistaken, he did two years and was placed on three years unrestricted probation. The criminal justice system just became a justice system when you had money and connections. The justice was "Just us" those who could afford to do heinous things and not have to do time for those crimes. He took out a large sweatshirt, sweatpants, a skull cap, and heavy socks from the suitcase. He would put on a hoodie to top everything off. He had been running the same route for months and it took him approximately an hour and fifteen minutes to run five miles. He used to be able to do the five miles in an hour, but as he aged it took him longer, He placed all his clothes on and headed for the door. He looked for his son's keys. That was something else he needed to do, get a set of keys made. He also had to manage to get employment. He was sure the Judge could assist him. He remembered that his son would always drop them on top of the television for some reason. He walked over to the living room and picked up the keys and out the door he went. As he climbed the 5-6 steps it took to get to the landing and out the front door, his mind started to drift again.

The Judge drank his wine and was able to get a little more comfortable. He placed his belongings under the bed, his shoes and laid upon the mattress that was so thin, he could feel the springs coming through from the bed. There is no way he was going to spend five years in this miserable place. He would use all his contacts and all his juice that he had on other people to make sure he would not be spending all that time in this prison. His roommate seemed to be engrossed in his book. He laid down facing his roommate. Not that that would do any good if he wanted to take advantage of him or steal any of his stuff. He was used to being the Master in his relationships with young men, but he had a feeling that if Jerome wanted to take advantage of him, there would be nothing he could do and maybe he would not want to stop him. He fell asleep thinking about the possibility of having an intimate relationship with Jerome for the time that he would spend in this horrible place. And if that happened, he would make it worth Jerome's while.

Jerome hit the pavement and decided to run to Eugenia's apartment, knock on the door and ask her how she was doing. It was about eight blocks to Eugenia's apartment. He was surprised to see her car parked outside on the street. He wondered if she had company. But according to local news reports, her man had been in a shootout in SE and was hospitalized or he thought that was him. He would double check the news when he returned to his son's apartment. He went down the driveway as the entrance to Eugenia's apartment was from the back. He stood outside of the apartment for a few minutes before he ran up the steps and knocked on the door. He knocked again and it seemed she was either not home or with someone. It was early, but he decided to be persistent and knocked again.

Eugenia sat straight up and went for her gun. Who the hell was knocking on the front door of the apartment? It must be someone with the wrong address. She got up, and jumped into her sweatpants, she looked around for a T-shirt, grabbed one, put on her slippers, made sure the gun was loaded and headed to the front door which was in the back of the apartment. Ila's apartment had two doors; Eugenia's only had one. The door knocking was persistent so maybe they were at the right door. It would not be the Company; she had no idea who it might be. She moved quickly to the window to see if she could get a glimpse of who was at the door. There he stood, the man from the wedding, what in the world did this man want. She walked to the door and stood on the side opposite the handle and screamed. "Who is it?" Jerome screamed back "It's Ancil Rogers." "And who is that?" Eugenia replied. "The brother from the wedding that rescued you." Jerome replied. "What do you want?" Screamed Eugenia. "I was just stopping by to make sure you were OK, that was some scene at the wedding two days ago. You good?" Eugenia hesitated, took the gun, and placed it down her bra, stepped slightly to the right, took the chain off the door, and released the dead bolt and opened the door. Oh no, she did not remember him looking so good, or maybe it was the sweat glistening off his face. "Good morning, Ancil, thank you for stopping by, yes I am fine." Jerome thinks quickly. "Can I interest you in a cup of coffee or hot chocolate at the local coffee shop?" Jerome said. Eugenia said, "hmmm that is an interesting proposition from a man who rescued me. Let me put warmer clothes on and I will meet you at the coffee shop in 15 minutes." Jerome nodded his head and said, "I will finish my run and meet you there in 15 minutes." Eugenia slowly closed the door, placed all the locks back in place and headed to the bathroom to brush her teeth, place a little makeup on, get her ankle gun, socks, tennis shoes, a heavy sweatshirt, and her bomber jacket. She removed the other gun from her bra and got dressed. She decided all she needed was ChapStick, a few dollars just in case and the keys to the apartment. She wondered if she would be able to find a skull cap, and there it was on the top closet shelf. The company did not miss anything. I guess they had done this type of thing so many times the checklist was tight. She would probably be placed on relocation of employees' duty while she was on maternity vacation— leave. She didn't even know what to call it. She got completely dressed, checked the apartment twice and went out the door. Stood at the top step for a few seconds, scanned the area then turned around to lock the deadbolt. She walked down the steps carefully as they were a little slippery. She hoped the new domicile would not have steps as she would be getting bigger. Once at the end of the steps she looked back at the apartments as she knew her time there was limited. She needed to get the word on Ila, but it was hard. The Company kept tight security on its employees even if you are an employee. She laughed, what she did know is that Ila was not dead and if she knew anything for sure, Ila was fighting her way out of whatever problem she was having at the hospital. As she walked up the driveway, she got a feeling someone was behind her. She did not hear footsteps, but a presence. She turned quickly only to see no one. She quickened her steps, not only for that reason, but it was chilly outside. She walked quickly to the corner, walked across the street from the coffee shop and looked around before crossing the street again to enter the shop. She walked in and Ancil was sitting at a back booth waiting patiently. Most people were standing in line to get coffee and bagels to go. There was only one waitress this time of the morning. The others came closer to lunch time. Eugenia walked to the booth and was nervous that Ancil sat facing the door. She thought of just sitting next to him but felt the booth was too small and that would be too intimate. She took a deep breath and slid into the booth. "Good morning again, have you ordered already," Eugenia said. "No, waiting on you, but that run has got me pretty hungry," Jerome replied. Before he could complete his sentence, the waitress was at the table. He was glad because he had no idea what his next words were going to be. "Morning my name is Sara, what can I get for you this morning." Jerome nodded to Eugenia, "I will have a cup of hot water with lemon and honey, two scrambled eggs, a plain bagel with cream cheese, and four pieces of bacon, crispy." "And you sir," Jerome had looked at the menu and really wanted something like steak and eggs with a large side of hash browns and coffee, but this was not that kind of place. He laughed in this head. "Thank you, I will have a bagel plain as well with hummus, four scrambled eggs, four pieces of bacon, water, light ice and coffee." The cream and sugar were on the table. The waitress thanked them for their order and walked away. There was a terrible three-minute silence. Jerome finally said, "So how are all of your friends, have you talked to them." Eugenia, "Tell me again how you got to be at the wedding." She was very cautious with this good-looking half breed sitting across the table from her. "I am Anthony Hollis' father. He goes to Georgetown and Ila was like a counselor to him on many occasions, not just an administrator. And as I understand it, she would give students food and money for food, if they needed it. I did not realize that he was in her office eating, drinking, and dumping his soul until after the wedding. He was very upset and still is over the entire ordeal. That is why I am asking about her now. I would like to tell him something when I return home. He is living with me until he finishes college, less expensive. Anthony has a different last name because I was well not around when he was born. Did not really want to be a dad at the time, but that is another story of which I am sure we will get to down the road." Eugenia thought to herself, down the road, this man does not understand that her down the road did not include him. There was more silence. Eugenia finally responded, "Well if I did not thank you for rescuing me that night what seems like forever ago, but was only three days ago, thank you sincerely." "You are most welcome," Jerome replied. Jerome laughed in his head. Those two years living with the Judge did him some good. He gave him a new language skill and now he was not always talking street. The waitress brought the drinks and a sample of a new cornbread they were going to try as a breakfast item. Broccoli cornbread with butter. As they both tried and loved the cornbread Jerome said, "So how is Ms.

Montgomery." Eugenia then opens the floodgates, telling him how concerned she was about her friends. How she had not heard anything. How she knew Stephen was dead but was not sure about Brock nor Ila's conditions and she was going to try to reach Paula today. This conversation took them straight through breakfast as the waitress brought the meal shortly after the drinks arrived and Eugenia talked the entire time. Jerome was surprised at her candor. He was also surprised to see that it looked like she was pregnant. There is a certain look about a woman when she is carrying a child. As she walked in, he felt she looked different. It was probably all his imagination, but.

The meal and the conversation had come to an end. Jerome asks the waitress for the check. She returned shortly and Jerome paid in cash of course. Before he went to prison, he made sure that his street money was placed into an account. His man "Short" transacted all the money and placed it into an account. Short said he made approximately $500,000 and got out of the game. Brought a home in Hyattsville, Maryland and started a trucking company. Jerome was super proud of him. When he got out, he contacted "Short" who gave him an ATM card to retrieve his money. He had no idea what that was. He gave him the pin number and in the account was $200,000. Now he knows that Short made more than that but was grateful for the funds to start his life again. Jerome asked Eugenia if she minded him walking her home. Eugenia told Jerome that she would rather walk alone. They rose and walked together towards the door. Eugenia gave Jerome a hug and thanked him for breakfast. Jerome said, "Can we do this again soon." Eugenia replied, "I will be moving soon. This is probably our last encounter, but I do thank you." "Really, Jerome said, I thought we were getting along great, I would really like to see you again." Eugenia replied, it is so complicated, it would take a lifetime to unravel the shit in my life, but again, thank you very much." She turned and walked away. Jerome stood in front of the coffee shop for a minute and thought," What the fuck do I do now." He decided to run after her. He started jogging towards her. Eugenia heard the fast footsteps approaching and stopped and stood against the wall of a building, as she wanted to make sure it was friendly footsteps, she turned and saw him running towards her. He stopped in front of her and said, "it's just a walk home, that is all to make sure you get there safely." Eugenia nodded her head and they walked silently to her apartment.

Carlton Watson stood across the street wondering who the fuck was Eugenia having breakfast with. Just because she was pregnant and being moved to a new location does not mean the Company forgot about the two dead bodies in the hotel room. Once she delivers this baby, she is going to have a lot of explaining to do. He walked slowly on the other side of the street making sure that whoever this man was he delivered Eugenia to her apartment safe and sound. His beeper went off and gave him an address to a new location to meet another agent on another case. He would circle back to Eugenia. He had a feeling that this guy was going to show up again and then he could get additional details. In the meantime he would take pictures with his camera (Mr. Snap) always had a camera.

It was getting dark, and Paula and Ila had to go into the house, but Sharon was still in the alley way with Mickey. Ila's poor heart was broken. It was the weekend, so that was something to look forward to.

It was a typical weekend. Everyone did their chores before coming outside. We all went to the basketball court to watch the boys. Ila had to take her little brother. She was not happy about it, but that only meant she could stay out later because no one gets in trouble if they have their baby brother along. Ila just laughed. If her baby brother was on the playground, he could care less where Ila was, but she knew better than to keep him out of her sight. Ila was looking for Paula, she was afraid to go to the house just in case they were supposed to be together. The crew went to the basketball court, hung out and got snacks from the corner store. Ila had a soda for Christopher so when he came off the court, he would have something to drink. Ila was shocked as they walked towards the pavilion close to the court, there Mickey was in the pavilion across the park sitting there with music playing from his boombox. Sharon almost peed on herself. "Ila, you see Mickey over there, I am going to go talk to him, I will see you guys later." Ila had a knot in the pit of her stomach. Her little brother had already run to the playground. She walked over to the playground and sat on the bench so that she could keep an eye on him. The others went under the pavilion to wait for their picks to come off the court. Christopher finished in about 10 minutes and came to sit on the bench with Ila. She really liked him, but they were around the same age and now he seemed so immature compared to Mickey. Christopher and Ila made a date to meet at the movies in Homewood next weekend. Ila would have to convince her crew to go, because dating was out of the question until she turned sixteen, according to her parents. The crew finished up there day at the courts and dreaded the long walk home, she was glad she brought the umbrella stroller for her little brother because he was tired and did not want to walk, even though he was too big for the stroller, it was better than trying to get him to walk all the way home.

It was dinner time and still no Paula. Ila sat on the steps in front of her house after dinner and then she saw Paula walking up the street towards her house. She came up the steps and sat down. "Where you been all day?" Ila asked. "With Sugarbear," Paula replied. "Did you use a condom, "Ila asked. "Yes, he did but he said the condom was so uncomfortable he took it off," replied Paula. Ila looked at Paula like she had two heads. "Are you crazy, you are going to get pregnant messing around with this older man and then what. We are fourteen about to be fifteen, what are you going to do with a baby." Paula looked at Ila and said, "I think I am in love with him." Ila looked at Paula and just nodded her head. "Paula we were supposed to only be having fun, not falling in love. You can't be in love with him, he could get in big trouble having sex with you as you are still a minor. Please don't do it again. I will ask my older brother to give me some condoms and you can carry your own." Paula looked excited and said, "Yes that would be a great idea." They sat on the porch until the streetlights came on. Paula said her goodbyes. Tomorrow was Sunday, so she would see her in Sunday school and Church. Ila did not bother to tell her that Sharon had run off with Mickey once again.

Weeks had gone by. Ila saw Mickey but he did not engage in conversation, just "Hello, how are you doing." Ila had stopped being crushed as Christopher had stepped up and they had gone to the movies. Swimming at Highland Park. Long walks in the bottoms of Frick Park and bus rides to East Liberty to the arcade. Christopher said he saved up his allowance for us to do certain things. Ila was not sure this was true, or that his parents were upper middle class and just gave him money. Ila really did not care where he got the money from because she benefited. Ila's family could not afford an allowance but were given benefits. Additional TV time, special treats from the store, more hours outside. Ila enjoyed those perks and never complained. Three months after Ila had introduced Paula to Sugarbear, they were still hot and heavy. Ila did not see her friend as often and Sugarbear was now picking her up and driving her to school. Ila really missed her friend, but knew that if they happened to break up, she would be there for the fall out. They still hung out in school and had several classes together. She did notice that Paula had gained a little weight and was not taking gym classes anymore. She said the Doctors had given her an excuse because of her asthma flare up so that she could take a study hall. Ila also noticed that Paula had not been talking about her cramps.

Then one Friday evening sitting on the steps Paula said. "I have not had my period for two months." Ila turned and looked at Paula with tears in her eyes. "Have you told Sugarbear," Ila asked. Paula began to cry "Yes, he wants me to get an abortion because if anyone finds out he will go to jail." Ila grabbed her friend by the hand and had no idea what their next steps were going to be but for tonight, they were both going to cry.

On Saturday morning, Ila set out to find Mickey. She left the entire crew on the block and headed to all the familiar places. First to the barber shop on Rosedale, then to the Tioga Café, onto the Honey Dew, circle back to the corner store and there he stood. Ila did not know why she did not start there. He started to smile as she walked up to him. She could not help but start to smile also. "Hello beautiful," he said. "Hi Mickey, can we talk," Ila responded. "Sure, come to my office." With that Mickey began to walk towards the alleyway. She knew if anyone saw her follow him to the alleyway it would be all over town, but this was an emergency. She followed behind him and as he entered the alleyway, there was a small path that someone had made to the left, he turned there and walked inside for about a quarter of a block and there was another opening. He had chairs set up and a tent. Is this where he lived, I thought, or is this where he took advantage of young women. Nevertheless, this conversation had to happen, and it had to happen today. Mickey used a napkin to wipe off the chair that Ila was about to sit down in. Ila sat silent for a moment. "Mickey, Paula is pregnant." "Pregnant, are you sure, I am positive my cousin used condoms. "I gave him some," Mickey said. "You gave him some, but he never used them," Ila replied. "So how pregnant is she," Mickey said. "About two months or more," Ila replied. "I will take her to planned parenthood and get her tested. I have a friend that works there, she will take care of everything." Ila looked at Mickey and started to cry. She was sad that she got Paula into this mess with Sugarbear. She never thought that it might come to this. Mickey got up and gave Ila a napkin to wipe her tears. He looked at her and remembered how good it was to have his dick in her ass and how willing her ass was to receive him. Just the thought of it made his dick hard. Ila looked up at Mickey and saw his dick was hard and her panties were wet instantly. So, this is how it all happens again and again. Ila was amazed at the thought that her body did things without any stimulation. He stood over her to make sure she saw how hard his dick was. She looked up at him with tears in her eyes and he reached down and stood her up and began to kiss the tears away. He slowly moved his hands down her thigh and made his way from her jumper to her panties, while kissing her deeply. He carefully pulled down her panties in the front and placed two fingers into her pussy. She loved the sensation and did not want it to stop. She eagerly accepted the fingers and began to kiss him passionately. He whispered in her ear, let me make love to you in the open air like we did in the apartment. Ila wanted to say no, but her body said yes. He released her and went to the other side of the tent and got a blanket and laid it down on the grass. Ila was sure this was where he brought Sharon, but at this point she did not care. All she wanted was to please this man so that he could do it to her again and again. He came back, took Ila's hand and guided her to the blanket. He slowly removed her panties and asked her to please lay on the blanket faced down and ass up. Ila did as he commanded. Once on the blanket face down, he raised her ass and began to lick it on the outside, rubbing it gently and then smacking it lightly. He opened her ass and began to lick it slowly. Ila could feel her ass opening to receive whatever he was going to place in it. He took his tongue and stroked it into her ass hole and Ila began to moan and then a light scream, it felt so good. He reached into his man purse that was lying by the other chair and pulled out Vaseline and a condom. He took a large portion of the Vaseline and placed it into the hole of Ila's ass and placed one finger in slowly, then two fingers. Ila's ass began to shake. She could not believe that after only one time, she was ready to receive him again. Mickey dropped his pants to his ankles and began stroking his dick. It was so hard you could see the veins from the base to the head popping out. He could not wait to get his dick in this sweet young ass. He pulled his two fingers out and could see the ass juices coming from Ila. He slowly opened her ass with one hand and guided his dick into her ass headfirst. Very slowly. Ila began to moan; this was a better sensation than last time. This time it almost felt like eating her favorite ice cream. The way it went down your throat and into the pit of your stomach and exploded. Mickey guided his dick slowly. Ila began to moan more. He put it in very little at a time. Her ass opened like a blooming rose. He could see the hollow and that is when he jammed her. Ila screamed with pleasure. Mickey stroked her ass back and forth; he could feel her tightening her butt muscle. "Stop that," Mickey screamed. "You are going to make me cum." Ila thought, so that is the secret. She began moving her butt muscle more and more and then she heard a primal scream come out of Mickey's throat. She began to laugh to herself, so this is how it is done. Mickey pulled out and let his semen ooze into the condom. Ila collapsed. This was a new feeling. She was not sure how to feel about what had just happened, but she hoped it would happen again and again. Mickey took napkins and wiped her ass and gently put her panties back on. Ila laid there for about 10 minutes as her knees hurt and so did her butt. She then repeated to Mickey, "Paula is pregnant, what are we going to do." Mickey replied, "I will take care of it. On Friday we will go to Planned Parenthood and confirm the pregnancy. If she is pregnant, I know a lady on Frankstown who can give Paula an abortion. Sugarbear will have to come up with the money. I think it is about $300.00." Ila got up, straightened her clothes, and he kissed her passionately. Ila walked back out to the alleyway, looking both ways to make sure no one was coming. What she did not know was that Sharon was lurking in the bushes and had seen and heard everything. Sharon was furious, she ran from behind the bushes to the tent and started hitting Mickey, telling him what a motherfucker he was, how could he fuck her good friend, she thought she was the only girl for him. Mickey let her swing on him several times and then grabbed her hands and led her to the chair. She was crying and screaming. Mickey bent over and whispered into her ear "Shut the fuck up before I slap the shit out of you. You know I can hurt you, so be a good girl and shut the fuck up." Sharon instantly dried her tears, she knew how brutal he could be when he got mad, but she was just so hurt. Mickey went and sat in the other chair, reached into his man purse, and got a joint. He lit it and looked around for his small cooler that had cokes and beer. It seemed too early to have a beer, but this little bitch was getting on his nerves. He took out a cold beer and twisted the cap and took a huge swig. Sharon was sitting in the chair silent. She knew that he would not beat her but bite her and put his entire fist up in her ass if he got mad. She was going to tell Ila to leave her man alone and to stick with little boys like Christopher. Mickey looked at Sharon and waved her over to his lap. Sharon got up wiping tears away and sat on Mickey's lap. He gave her a swig of beer and a couple hits off the joint. He whispered in her ear how she was the only one and that Ila had wanted to talk to him about one thing that led to another, but it would never happen again. She knew what Ila wanted to talk to him about. Ila and Paula always acted like goodie two shoes when all along those girls were whoring around just like her, only she got money. Sharon laughed to herself. The secret is out, and she will hold it until she needs it. She took the joint out of Mickey's mouth and pulled on it several times. It was good weed, and it did not take her long to place his hand up her dress. She had on panties, but he immediately moved the panties aside and placed his fingers in her vagina. This is what Sharon loved the best. This is how Mr. Burns taught her how to cum. She moved Mickey's hand to the right spot and Mickey began to laugh as she came on his fingers. It felt like pee. It was so good. Mickey could no longer contain himself. Even though he had just come minutes ago, his dick was hard again and ready to penetrate something. He licked his fingers and put the fire out on the tip of the joint and placed it on top of his beer bottle. This little girl was an expert at sucking dick. That old man had taught her well. He would even give her a couple of dollars to buy whatever her little heart desired. He tapped her on the ass to get up off his lap and to sit on the chair. He got on his knees, pulled down her panties and began to eat her like a savage dog. Sharon's eyes rolled in the back of her head. She knew that this sensation would make her forgive anything that he had done to her. He licked her thighs, legs, lifted her legs to lick her ass hole and came back to her vagina. Sharon moaned with pleasure and then he stopped, picked up napkins, wiped her off, pulled up her panties and told her to have a wonderful day and he did not want to hear anything more from her about Ila. He gave her five dollars and told her to get lost.

Ila walked up the alley and she knew by the time she got back to the house the street would be filled with people and children. And, Paula would be wondering where she was. Those 30 minutes with Mickey seemed unreal but it was not. What an introduction to sex, it was not like in the movies but after this second time, she could probably get used to the sensation. She laughed. Paula was sitting on the steps waiting for Ila. She looked so sad. Ila walked up the steps and sat down. Ila's grandmother was sitting in the porch swing. She always sang a song under her breath and Ila had no idea what she was singing. But it was soothing so we all just sat and listened. Three girls from Hamilton Hill were walking down the street. They all went to Crescent High School. They looked like they wanted trouble. Ila and Paula got really tense, but if they wanted a fight, they were going to get it. They walked past the house, called us trolls and kept walking. They must have known not to try to come up on the porch, Grandma had a big bat waiting for someone to try some shit. Ila and Paula laughed until they started to cry. They stopped laughing and decided to walk up to the basketball court in Belmar Gardens. They were just about to go down the street to get Sharon when she came walking out of the alleyway with a box of donuts and three yahoos. Ila and Paula were happy to see the food and the yahoo drinks. They both had not eaten breakfast. Paula looked like she had not gotten any sleep, but sometimes, that is just how she looked. They sat on the porch and ate and forgot all about walking to the basketball court. They started playing jacks. Yes, they were too old to be playing jacks, but they all enjoyed trying to beat one another. After about an hour Sharon said she was going home to check in. She walked down the steps and truly looked tired. Ila ran after her. "Hey, Ila screamed, what is wrong with you today." Sharon did not respond. Are you upset about something? Sharon nodded her head no. "So, what is the problem?" Ila replied. "I think I got something," Sharon said. "Got something, what do you mean got something?" Sharon replied, "my pee pee hurts, and it burns when I pee." "Your pee pee, what is that your pussy? Good God Sharon, pee pee." Ila replied. "Well, that was the only word I could think of." They both laughed. They walked to her house in silence. "OK, take a bath in Epsom salt today and tomorrow and see how you feel on Monday. We will cut class and go to the health department; my Aunt Phyllis works there, and she will take care of everything." Sharon started jumping up and down and then she remembered seeing her fucking Mickey. She started to cry. "Ila, why are you having sex with my boyfriend?" "Boyfriend, who you talking about," Ila said.

"Mickey." Sharon screamed. Ila looked down at the ground. "So here is the plan, if you are not feeling better, we will go to homeroom, second and third period and then walk to the health department during lunch. We can go out the side door where Man Man, sits and he will let us in and out." Sharon nodded her head and walked up the steps to her house. Ila stood on the sidewalk and could feel her butt start to hurt. Oh no, she hoped her ass was not going to start hurting like Sharon's pee pee. She laughed in her head. What a day it had been already. Ila walked back to the porch and sat with Paula. She looked so sad. "Let's go to the movies. Let me see if my mother will let me go." Ila said. "You got money." Ila asked Paula. Paula shook her head no. Ila had five dollars, which would get them in the movie, share popcorn and a large soda. Ila got up and went into the house to ask permission to go to the movies. Her mother was in the kitchen preparing to cook dinner. Ila stood in the kitchen archway waiting to get her mother's attention. Her mother looked up from peeling potatoes and singing that same song that grandma sang under her breath. "Hi, where have you been and why did you leave the house so early," her mother said. "I had to run to Aunt Florence's house to help her put some clothes in boxes that she cannot wear anymore. Someone from the Church was coming to pick them up." "Well, I was about to call the police and was going to have your dad whip that ass, but Ila you are draining, and, in my heart, I knew you were OK," her mother said. "You look like you want something. You need something to drink?" her mother said. "No mom, I want to go to the movies with Paula to see Mothra vs Godzilla," Ila said. Her mother looked at her.

"You got money?" said her mother. "Yes, I have five dollars from helping Aunt Florence for the last two weeks," said Ila. "Streetlights come on at 7:00 p.m. I will explain to your father why you are not at dinner. Ask grandma for one of her watches because if the movie is not over by 6:30 p.m. you better get your tail up and start walking fast towards this house, are we clear," Ila's mother said. "Clear," said Ila. Ila screamed thank you as she ran out the kitchen, through the dining room and up the steps (all 16) to her bedroom. She went into her closet and in a shoe box was her secret hiding place. She had about ten dollars because Aunt Florence insisted on paying her for every little job she did and Ila was glad because this gave her money for French fries, or a fruit off the lunch line at school. Her family was on the food program, and you could only get certain items off the food line on the program. She recounted her one-dollar bills to make sure no one had found her hiding place. She put the money back in a sock and placed the sock in a shoe and put the lid on the box. She ran down the other hallway to ask her grandmother for a watch and instead of getting out of her rocker, she took her Timex off and handed it to Ila. "Lose my Timex, don't come home," her grandmother said. Ila securely placed the watch halfway up her arm just to make sure. She ran back to her room and got sweaters for her and Paula just in case. She placed the money in her sock and ran back down the hallway and down the steps two at a time. When she hit the porch, Paula was in the bushes, throwing up. Shit! She ran back into the house, up the steps to the bathroom, took a handful of toilet paper and stuffed it down her bra and ran back down the steps and out the door to the side of the house. The throw up smelled horrible. It was the yahoo and donuts they had eaten earlier. She gave the toilet paper to Paula and waited for her to stand completely upright. Ila looked at her. She was lighter than she was before. Ila began to laugh, and Paula began to laugh. She wiped her face; Ila gave her a sweater and they started walking to the theater which was on the corner of Bennett and Homewood Avenues.

The walk to her apartment was meaningfully silent. When they got to the driveway Jerome hesitated. Eugenia looked at him and said, why the hesitation. Jerome said, "I think this is far enough. I will check on you again tomorrow. I am going to spend most of the day with my son as I took time off work to be with him and to attend the wedding. I am not due back to work until January 10. "Would you like to come and have a cup of tea." Eugenia asked. "No," Jerome replied, "I am going on to the house to take a shower and spend time with my son. Oh, by the way do you have children, Eugenia," Jerome asked. "I am about too," replied Eugenia and she began walking down the driveway. Jerome decided that the gentlemanly thing to do would be to make sure she got into her apartment safely. He trotted to catch up with her. Jerome looked at the back of Eugenia and could imagine her high ass in his face. He shook his head and caught up with her and walked in silence to the bottom of the steps. He watched as she took the steps slowly and it seemed to him, she had put an extra twitch in her step. He laughed inside. She had no idea he would wax that ass if she let him. She placed the key in the door and walked inside without looking back. He turned and ran up the driveway and made his way back to the apartment. His son was just moving around and asked his dad if he wanted to go to breakfast. His father said, "I will make you breakfast, give me 30 minutes. Jerome went into the kitchen, pulled out two eggs, bacon, and frozen hash browns. As he was preparing the breakfast he went to the phone on the wall and dialed the Judge's number. "Hello, how may I help you," the Judge said. "Hey Judge, this is Jerome, I wondered if the paperwork we prepared was ready for pickup," Jerome said. "Yes, it can be picked up at the law office of Pennington and Pennington in Arlington, Virginia. The receptionist has the package," It will be necessary for me to see you again to complete the transaction. I will be at a wedding at the Georgetown Inn on Sunday at 2:00 p.m., please come by and sign the additional paperwork," the Judge said. And the phone went dead. Jerome looked at the phone in his hand and knew the unfinished business was a dick up the Judge's ass. Jerome would have to get in touch with one of his gay boys that had gotten out and was hanging out in SE DC. He had taken care of the Judge while he was in prison. He had a young gay inmate visit the Judge once a week. The Judge received mail with cash money in it every two weeks in an unopened envelope. Jerome would go to SE on Sunday and find his boy Cash; he had been out for about 3 months, and he was the Judge's favorite while he was incarcerated. If picking up Cash weekly is what it took to get all his paperwork done and done correctly, well up the ass with Cash it will be. Jerome knew that the Judge had something to do with his early release and he was grateful but not to the point where he would give him some of his dick. But he would supply him with dick anytime he needed it. Jerome turned on the stove to 325 and placed the hash brown on a cookie sheet. He was not hungry but placed a bit more on it just for him. It would take about 20 minutes for the hash browns. He broke the eggs and placed them in a bowl. He added a little sugar, salt and pepper and a little garlic salt and whipped them up till they were foamy. He placed the bacon next to the hash browns on the sheet and placed it in the oven. He put the hash browns on foil in the hope that the bacon grease would not penetrate. He laughed, that never worked in the prison kitchen, he knew it would probably not work here either. He sat and thought about what his next move was going to be. He had to win the confidence of Eugenia. He could not say much because he did not know what his background was going to be and he was grateful that during breakfast, Eugenia was comfortable talking about herself today, so Jerome did not have to say much. But he was sure that their next encounter would be different. He could hear Anthony finally moving around again. "Anthony, you ready for me to put the eggs on," he yelled. Anthony replied, "Give me 10 minutes, I am going to hop in the shower." "Son, we have to make a run, so dress for the outdoors please," Jerome replied. Anthony jumped in the shower. He was in constant fear for his dad's life. His mother was in S.E. somewhere in a crack house. Some days he felt very defeated. But today he was going to enjoy the day with his father and try to forget about the past. He wanted to finish at Georgetown and become an engineer. He was fascinated with buildings, structures, the environment, etc. He could not wait to make legitimate paper, as his father would call it. He showered, dressed, and yelled from the bedroom to his father that he could put the eggs on, to please put cheese in the eggs. Jerome opened the refrigerator, he thought he saw cheese, but was not sure. But there it was on the door. He got the cheese and cut up small chunks into the egg bowl and whipped them once again. The eggs cooked fast, and the bacon and hash browns were done. His son did not eat a lot of bread. So, toast was not necessary. Anthony strolled in wearing Georgetown gear from head to toe and tennis shoes and sat at the small table and chairs in the corner of the kitchen. His father served him breakfast. He really liked living with his father. Not only just to get to know him but he liked to cook, and Anthony did not. His father brought his plate to the table with a tall glass of orange juice. His father stood at the sink and ate his hash browns. "I'm going to take a quick shower and then if you don't mind, off to Arlington, VA. I promise not to keep you in the street all day," Jerome said to his son. Anthony replied, "I have heard that story before." They both laughed.

Eugenia came into the apartment, took off all her clothes at the foot of the bed and fell across the bed and went to sleep. This baby has not allowed her to have much activity lately. Seems all she wanted to do was eat and sleep and she was very horny. She got up out of the bed, picked up her clothes and folded them as in three days they would be coming to get everything. She missed Ila. She knows she was really her protector, but Ila always had something going on she did not have to worry about entertainment cause Ila was the entertainment queen, always into some shit. She pulled a t-shirt from a box, found her slippers, and walked to the kitchen; it was time to eat again. As she walked to the door, there was a quick knock, and an envelope was pushed under the door. She moved quickly to the window wanting to see who was responsible for all the envelopes. All she saw was a bike courier riding away. She should have known that that would be the way the Company would deliver envelopes. No car, no license plates, make or model of car, instead what type of bicycle was it and what was the person wearing on the bike. Well in DC there were a thousand bike couriers and tracking one of them down would be hard unless you caught them on camera from start to finish. She reached down to retrieve the envelope and walked to the kitchen. She sat down to open the envelope when her stomach started to turn. She stood up and went to the sink and heaved but nothing came up. She grabbed a glass and ran the water from the sink, filled the glass and began to sip on it slowly. She needed to eat again. She went to the refrigerator and decided to have bacon and eggs again. There was smoked salmon, cream cheese and bagels in the refrigerator also. Eugenia settled for the quickest, smoked salmon, cream cheese, and a bagel with a cup of green tea. Suddenly, she could not wait to eat. She placed the kettle on for hot water, reached back into the fridge and got a lemon for the tea and pulled out the smoked salmon, cream cheese, and bagel. She laid everything out like a smorgasbord. She went to the kitchen drawer and got a knife, spoon, and fork. Reached into the drainer and got a plate. She cut open the package of smoked salmon and began slicing the meat into small slices so that they could be placed on the bagel. For some odd reason, she went back into the fridge and got a block of cheese. She took the cheese and sliced pieces onto the plate. If she was not pregnant, this would never be a meal. She laughed again. It was so quiet in the apartment, she went to the bedroom and turned the radio to WHUR, it was a great radio station. She turned it up loud so that she could hear the music in the kitchen. She began to eat salmon and cheese. The kettle was screaming. Her stomach said, don't stop eating. She laughed again. Got up to make tea so that it would be warm not hot after she ate. Left the tea bag in the water probably longer than she should have. Took it out and placed it on the kitchen counter in a saucer. Took the cup to the table and began eating again. She cut the bagel and sliced it into four pieces so it would last longer and spread cream cheese over each piece. She ate slowly but steadily in silence. Then that damn phone rang and scared the shit out of her. She always forgot there was a phone in the apartment. All her communication came from her beeper. She got up and rushed to the phone. She picked up the receiver and said "Yes," The voice on the other end said, "Change in plans. Then she looked at the receiver in her hand. Tomorrow, dang, she wondered why this was placed into Defcon 5. She replaced the receiver in the cradle. Shit, she thought, she did not read what was in the envelope. It would probably explain the urgency of getting her out of the apartment. She walked back to the kitchen and looked at the envelope; really, she wondered what could have happened. She sat down and slowly opened the envelope: Inside the letter read, the investigation into the bodies found at the Marriott hotel has increased and with your prints being found on the tape cassette, you are being looked at as a suspect from other agencies. Our people are still on the case, and we are reframing the case to murder and suicide of lovers. No new information will be forthcoming without contacting the families of these individuals. Be prepared to move by noon tomorrow and be sure to destroy this communication and all other communication given to you in envelopes before you leave this apartment. A cleaning crew will come in once your belongings have been taken out of the apartment. Your new apartment will be completely furnished. You have already received the keys to your car and the apartment. Once your things have been removed, please arrive at the new apartment by 2:00 p.m., you will be given further instructions at that time. Ms. Montgomery will be housed in the apartment adjacent to yours as she is still in danger. There will be another agent assigned to cover both of you as your condition will not allow you to be an active agent. Currently she is in a private room at Walter Reed with a guard. FYI, Officer Waters has been released and will have to undergo extensive rehabilitation, six months is the estimated timeframe. Agent Brock is in a coma and is still in intensive care. Eugenia sat and the tears began to flow. She did not tell Franklin that she was pregnant. She was going to tell him right after the wedding, but then the shit hit the fan. She will have given birth before he is recovered. There would be no way she would be able to see him. She will have to find a way to tell him about the baby particularly after the baby is born. She did not want her baby to grow up without a father. Things were not going as she had planned. Nothing in this business ever does. She sat in the kitchen until day became night, just thinking about possible next steps. Around 6:00 p.m. she snapped out of it. She would have to take this thing one day at a time. She got up and cleaned off the table and washed the dishes. Her tea had gotten cold. She poured it down the drain and put the kettle on to make another cup. This was a day that having a drink would be just what the Doctor ordered, but not in her condition. She went to the side drawer of the kitchen to find scissors. She walked to the living room to retrieve the other envelope and took it back to the kitchen. The kettle started to scream again. She made another cup of tea and sat and cut up the typed messages into tiny pieces of confetti. She was going to burn the pages in the sink but decided that the cutting up of the messages would be therapy for her. After cutting the messages up into tiny pieces, she placed them into a garbage bag and took the bag and placed it in one of the boxes that was supposed to be picked up. She laid out her Georgetown sweat suit, tennis shoes, ankle gun, socks, bra, and panties. Placed other guns in their cases with the safety on and placed them in a backpack. She went to the bathroom and put all her toiletries into a small box. She would place this box, guns, and other paraphernalia in the car in the morning. She took the small box to the bedroom and went back to the bathroom to take a shower. She looked at her face in the mirror. It was amazing how she had filled out in three months. Her breasts were hurting, her hair was growing like crazy, her bras did not fit, and her thongs were out of the question. She would have to buy all new underwear soon.

Anthony and Jerome finished breakfast and headed out the door. They had to get to Arlington to get Jerome's identity papers from the law office. Traffic in DC was always terrible. They were making their way to the 14th street bridge. Once across the bridge the traffic in Virginia was lighter. They headed to the law office listening to WHUR. Anthony parked and looked at his father and said "do I have time to run down the street and get a pair of tennis shoes. It is right down the street." Jerome looked at his son and said, "This is going to take less than 10 minutes, and then we can head to the store." I do have to go to the ATM to get some cash." Jerome jumped out of the car and entered the building. The floors shined so bright you could have eaten off them. The receptionist was very polite. "How can I help you?" "Hello, I am here to pick up an envelope from Judge Pennington." "Yes sir, I have the envelope right here." She handed the envelope to Jerome. She was told not to ask this man any questions. Just hand him the envelope. Confidentiality was extremely important in this position, so no questions were asked. The gentleman was good looking and built extremely well. "Sir is there anything else you need," the young lady said. Jerome looked up and smiled, it was the way she said it. "No, thank you, this is exactly what I need," Jerome replied. Jerome turned and headed towards the door. If she had given him that kind of door opener 20 years ago, he would be banging her in the men's room by now. He laughed out loud and opened the door. His son sat patiently in the car. Jerome jumped back into the car and told his son he was ready to go. His son was an excellent driver. Anthony knew what was in the envelope but could not know the particulars. If they ever were separated and he had to answer questions, he would have none of the answers. He could not wait to get a new pair of tennis shoes. He had gotten his check from the University for financial aid. He was going to be thrifty, but he really wanted these tennis shoes. As he drove up to the store, he asked his father if he was coming in, his father said "No, but please pick me up a pair of tennis shoes, black and white, size 11. You make the choice, it does not matter to me. I will give you the money back when I go to the ATM." Anthony nodded his head. Jerome started going through his paperwork. New license Ancil Jerome Rogers, same birth date, birth certificate, SE DC, passport, work ID for Georgetown Prep as a maintenance officer for 15 years, keys to a car that was parked at the law office, they would have to go back to get the car. Also in the envelope were keys to an apartment on Glebe Road in Arlington, first floor, apartment number one. He really did not want to be that far away from his son, but the apartment was being paid for by Pennington and Pennington as an executive relocation apartment. The apartment was completely furnished. All traces of Jerome Romi Rome Hollis were in the past. There was already a phone installed in the apartment and it had already been assigned a number. He would give Anthony the phone number but nothing else. He was also going to purchase beepers for both of them. Now they were digital which made it a little easier to communicate. But the cell phone, now that was what he really wanted, but on a maintenance man's salary, that would cause people's eyebrows to raise. The apartment was ready to move into. So, the plan was to move in on Monday, take care of the Judge on Sunday, and spend a quiet evening with his son tomorrow. He was sure his son was going to be glad to see him go. He had not had company male or female since he arrived. Not that Anthony was a social butterfly, but he had met many people on campus. But Anthony also understood that he could not develop long term relationships right now. After he graduated and started working for whomever, he could start developing a relationship. By that time Jerome would have been completely established and there would be no side eyes as to where he came from. Anthony understood the plan and was willing to sacrifice some of his life to make sure his dad was safe.

Anthony bounced out of the store happy with his purchases. He had brought two pairs for himself and one for his dad. He opened the back door of the car and placed the shoes on the back seat. He then returned to the driver's seat. He looked at his father and could sense that what was in the envelope was serious. "Anthony, I will be moving out on Monday to Arlington, and we must go back to the law office and pick up my car. Anthony nodded his head and headed back to the law office. He listened as his father explained that they would be getting pagers to keep in constant contact. As they drove into the parking lot, there sat a brand-new silver Ford Taurus. It was the first year for this car. Anthony started yelling, "Dad can I drive it, please." "Of course, let's park your car in the third row of cars, put the tennis shoes in the trunk and let's ride." They both got out of the car and headed towards the car. As soon as they got to the car the receptionist was leaving the office on lunch break. She looked at them both and walked swiftly to the car. She had seen the car when she came into work and wondered who it belonged to. She was hoping she would not get in trouble for walking over but all she wanted to do was sit in the car. She was driving a Ford Escort and it looked like her grandmother's car, but it ran well and required little maintenance. Jerome saw her approaching and swiftly got into the car. Anthony lingered outside of the car looking at the new slick look of the car. "Hi, there," Alicia said. This is a beautiful car. I work in the law office. I saw the car this morning and wondered who it belonged to." Anthony could not talk for a moment. He had not seen a girl on his campus that looked like this. He could feel his penis rising. He immediately turned around and faced the car. "Oh, yes my father brought it for me for my birthday, it was a surprise." "Wow," Alicia replied. "May I sit in it," she said. Anthony replied, "My Dad has an important meeting to get to, but we will come back after the meeting, and you can sit as long as you want." Alicia smiled, showing all her teeth. "Yes, that would be wonderful. See you when you return." She turned and walked swiftly to her Escort. Her hour lunch goes so fast when she had to go purchase lunch. She normally would have packed her lunch but woke up too late after being at the hospital with her brother. The family was taking turns spending time with him. He was about to go to a rehabilitation center. She did not know which one yet but visiting would be nicer. The rehab centers had better food and she could push him around in a wheelchair outside. "What she should have said to the young man, was "Hi my name is Alicia Waters, I am currently single and would love to ride in your car." But of course, she did not say that. She could kick herself in the head, he was so handsome. She really hoped they would return.

Anthony jumped in the car and looked at his father. They both laughed, he had taught him well in the little time they had spent together. He would make sure they would return after dark to get his car. But, dang it, he really would like to see her again, but it would not happen today, for sure. They drove to the ATM, had lunch, and headed to Glebe Road to check out the new apartment. The complex was huge. It had six different sections according to size, studios, one bedroom, jr. one bedroom, two bedrooms and two bedrooms with a balcony. They searched for the address 4832 #1. It was on the back side of the complex, which was perfect for Jerome. They found the address and got out of the car. The front door was locked. He took the keys out of the envelope he received. There were three keys on the ring. He inserted the first one and it worked. The Judge's people had thought of everything. But he wondered how much longer he had to supply the Judge with young gay boys. Jerome decided he would put the Judge in another compromising position, like getting him high and taking pictures of Cash putting a coke bottle up his ass or something of that magnitude and keep them. He would think of the perfect plan that would end that relationship. They entered the apartment. It had a very large main room, which was the living room, kitchen, and dining area. No walls in-between. Down a small hallway to the left was the bathroom and further down the hall was the bedroom. One large room with multiple windows that looked out to a wooded area. Jerome was not happy about that but understood that if he had to escape into the woods, it was right behind the apartment, so he thought that was smart. They walked back to the large room. He had missed the large closet that was at the front door to the right.

The main room had two large windows that looked out to the parking lot. Perfect. It did not have a lot of furniture, but it had enough in it for Jerome to move in and be comfortable. When you have spent the 15 years of your life in a cell that was seventy square feet and most of the time those cells had two people in them. If you were incarcerated in the 70's and early 80's the population was overwhelming with crack dealers, crack addicts and gangs. It was a miserable place and Jerome was going to make sure that Eugenia paid for sending him to prison for that amount of time. Without her testimony he probably would have done only five years. "Dad, Dad, can I move in with you? This is much bigger than my apartment. I can sleep in the living room area." Anthony said. Jerome snapped out of his head and replied. "Son, when you finish school, we will move into a house together. But for now, you can walk or ride your bike or drive to school. Living all the way in Arlington would not make sense. You are going into your second year. It won't be long, and we will move on with our lives." Anthony looked at his father and a knot began in his stomach. He felt that with his father's past, looking into the future with him should be something Anthony should look forward to but there were days when he wanted to just run away from his entire life and start over again somewhere else. But for right now he was going to enjoy the time they spent together. "Ok Dad, if I have a hot babe I want to impress, you will have to stay at my apartment, and we will come here. The least you can do is give me a key." Jerome laughed and said, "We will get you keys on the way back to DC. We will stop by the bank, get keys made at the hardware store and go have dinner." "Yeah Dad, you said we would not be out all day, and it is almost 4:00 p.m." Anthony said. They both laughed. They went into the kitchen to see if it was furnished with the necessities, and it was. Satisfied that he would enjoy this space, they left to finish their errands, pick up Anthony's car and return to Georgetown. Anthony was still thinking about Alicia. She was a babe that he would bring to this apartment.

Alicia returned from lunch and could not get that young man off her mind. She knew that his father's phone number was in the files, but that was against the rules to find out information for personal use with clients. She was hoping she would see them when they came to pick up the other car. She could not wait to tell her Uncle Frank about this new guy. Maybe she would wait because he would instantly have his background looked at. Yes, she would keep this crush a secret until she hopefully got to know him. She laughed in her head. Her brother was in rehabilitation after being shot at a police raid in Southeast. Yes, she would wait, but it brought a smile to her face at the possibility of being with that young man.

Mothra vs. Godzilla the movie was great. Ila and Paula were both screaming at the screen. They had seen most of the Godzilla movies. They walked out of the movie as the sun was going down. They began to walk fast because Ila did not want to be placed on punishment for arriving home after the streetlights were on. Ila and Paula reached home in record time. Paula went home reluctantly, and Ila walked home, screamed in the door that she was home and sat on the porch. She loved sitting in the swing or on a crate and watching and hearing the noise of the street. It was wonderful growing up on a block where everyone knew each other. You never went hungry and when your rent could not be paid, everyone pitched in to help. Ila had no idea how her world would go into a tailspin when her parents decided to move on up to a "So called" better neighborhood.

Sunday at church was the same each Sunday. Ila's grandmother would make sure everyone was up for Church. Jack would pile everyone into the car and drive to church and let everyone out and he would drive back home. Sometimes he would come back and get the family but most times the family took a jitney back to the house. Or Ila and her crew would walk back home. If they walked, they could stop by people's homes to see what was for dinner and get a little from every house so that by the time they got home they were full. They would take off their Church clothes immediately and meet back up on the porch in about an hour. At any given time, there were five to ten kids hanging on the porch, in the front yard, or just sitting on the steps. Jack did not mind because he knew where his kids were. It cost the family money to have that many kids around all the time, with ice cream, popsicles, one slice peanut butter sandwiches, etc., but he would have it no other way. His kids were safe from the streets and if he could shelter other kids, that was a great blessing. He would sit in the front room with the bay window and watch all that was going on.

Monday morning, the crew all met, headed to the donut shop, pulled their pennies and nickels together to get donuts on the way to school. Ila and Sharon were going to cut school so that they could go to the health department and Mickey and Paula were headed to planned parenthood to get her tested. Ila had asked her cousin Tomika to give her baby food jars for a science experiment. She had gone down the street on Sunday, gotten the jars and asked her to boil the jars because they had to be extra clean for the experiment. Her cousin cursed her and boiled the jars anyway. She loved her cousin. She smoked weed, worked at the local hospital as a receptionist and she knew everyone's business. She made good money and was married to a man who worked at the steel mill. They drove a Buick Riviera. He worked nights and she worked days, which was how most people survived on the street. Most did not want their kids to go to day care which was sparse and expensive. Ila was blessed because her grandmother was at the house most of the time, and when she was not, she was back shortly. The families had to work like well-oiled machines for everything to work out. Ila took the jars and dropped one at Paula's house and one at Sharon's house. She told them both to pee in the jar first thing in the morning and wrap in newspaper to keep warm and place in their backpacks and to make sure the lid was on tight. She had called her Aunt Phyllis on Sunday to get the instructions. She also said that if any of this had anything to do with Ila, she was going to bust her in the head. She loved her family. No sympathy, we just going to bust you in the head.

Ila was a little scared. She had so many relatives in the neighborhood if anyone saw her out of school, she would be grounded for sure. They all kind of walked to school in silence. The rest of the crew had no idea why everyone was so quiet, but they decided not to say a word. As we walked up to the school, Mickey was standing across the street because he and Paula were going to Planned Parenthood right after homeroom check in. He made sure everyone saw him including Sharon who just glared at him because she thought for sure he had given her something. We all went our separate ways. Paula and Ila went to homeroom, got checked in and when the bell rang, Paula went out the side door where Man-Man sat, and Ila and Sharon went on to their first and second classes. Sharon met Ila after her second class at the same door and Man-Man let them out wanting a quarter from both of them. Sharon gave him a dollar and said they wanted to be let back in before the lunch period was over so that they could go to their afternoon classes. Sharon also asks that they leave their books in his locker which was right next to his chair. He said that would be an additional dollar. Sharon gave him the dollar and they both dropped their books in the locker. This guy was making a fortune off poor kids, but he did not care. His job was on the line, and he was going to profit off children that did not want to go to school. Most of the juvenile detention officers were going to houses daily to check up on students. They did not really pay attention to those who came to school and left unless they were reported.

Paula met Mickey on the side of the school. Sugarbear was waiting in the car looking very nervous. Paula climbed into the back seat while Mickey jumped onto the passenger side. Sugarbear said hello in a nervous voice and Paula did the same. It was a long quiet ride to Planned Parenthood in East Liberty. The trio pulled into the parking lot and Mickey asked for the jar of pee. Paula took the jar out of her backpack and handed it to Mickey. He jumped out of the car and ran into the building. Sugarbear really did not know what to say. If people found out she was pregnant he could go to jail. "Paula, I am sorry I was so careless with you, your body, and your feelings. There is not much to say but, I wish you were 16 years old, we could get married and could have the baby," Sugarbear said. Paula could do nothing but cry. Sugarbear also started to cry. They sat quietly waiting for Mickey. Mickey was running back to the car. He jumped into the car and said, "It is going to take two hours, so we will take you back to school and I will come back and pick up the test," Mickey said. They both nodded their heads. Sugarbear had to go to work, so Mickey would take him to work after they dropped off Paula and Mickey would circle back to Planned Parenthood. The test was called a, hCG antibodies, and urine test. Mickey did not want to know all the particulars from his friend. He just wanted to know if Paula was pregnant. But because there were patients waiting to get abortions in the clinic, his friend had to explain the process. He also learned that an abortion was $350.00 cash. He asked his friend was there any way to shave some of that cost, she said no, but she would get the pregnancy test for free. Also, in case he did not know, Planned Parenthood is not legally allowed to give abortions to minors without parent consent and the parent must be here with the birth certificate of the minor. Mickey thanked her and told her he would be back in two hours. It was a long quiet ride back to the school. Paula got out of the car, went to shut the door, said goodbye and threw up in the grass. Sugarbear had put the car in park, he jumped out of the car to make sure she was alright. He had a rag in the car, which was not so clean, but it could be used to wipe her mouth and shirt. He was shaken to the core. He had fallen in love with Paula and there was not a damn thing that could be done. Paula thanked him and walked into the side door of the school where Man-Man was waiting to open the door. Mickey supplied him with weed, so there is not much he would not do for Mickey. She walked through the door slowly and he took one look at Paula and knew something was wrong. It was none of his business and he was not about to get into Mickey's business. He got up, pulled her books out of the locker, and gave them to her. Paula thanked him and went to the lunchroom. There was about 10 minutes left until her lunch period would be over. She went in and grabbed mash potatoes and surprise meat and bread. It was a surprise meat because no one knew what it was. She also got milk. She did not like milk, but for the time she was going to carry the baby she wanted to be good to it. She also knew that there was a crazy gene in her family so it would be best for her to never have children. She found a seat and ate quickly and went to her next class.

Ila and Sharon walked the five blocks to the Health Department. Ila had let her aunt know that they were coming around lunch time. They entered the health department. Ila asked for her Aunt Phyllis. They waited about five minutes and Aunt Phyllis came to the desk. She walked around the desk and started walking towards the door. Ila and Sharon followed. They walked to the lady's bathroom. Aunt Phyllis asked for the urine sample. Sharon reached in her backpack and handed the jar to her wrapped in newspaper. She told them that it would be a few hours. "Ila, come by the house after school and I will give you the results of the test," her aunt said. Ila nodded her head, and they all left the bathroom. Sharon and Ila walked back to school in silence for a couple of blocks. Ila finally said. "Since when is Mickey your boyfriend?" Sharon said, "We have been together a lot, we have had sex." "OK, so since when is Mickey your boyfriend, is Mr. Burns your boyfriend?" Sharon looked at Ila and began to cry "You know that is for money, my family is poor, you have everything," Sharon replied. Ila looked at her like she had two heads; this girl had smoked too much weed. "If it is going to make you this unhappy, I will not be with Mickey again, but I really like him and he was after me first, you took it upon yourself to have sex with him."

"You don't have to have sex with men for money Ila, you have no idea what it is like to never have money," Sharon screamed to the top of her lungs. Ila began to walk fast because she was going to slap the shit out of Sharon. We all live on the same street, we are all broke, or just making it. The only difference is that I have both my parents and my grandmother, and our household loves each other. So, I don't get no dick because of that. She's crazy. Ila decided she would be very careful with Mickey so that Sharon would not find out. But that man had opened her ass and her mind to sex, and she liked it. She was not going to get pregnant if he had sex in her butt, and she did not mind. They ran to the side door and Man-Man let them in. They got their books and went to their next class. They had missed lunch; Ila's stomach was empty. She walked into her class and went to sit next to Paula. She looked really light. Ila wondered if she had been throwing up again. When

Ila sat down, Paula handed her a snicker's bar with the wrapper already undone halfway. Ila smiled at her friend; she knew they had missed lunch. The lights went dim, they were in science class and today they were watching a movie on dissecting frogs, which is something they would have to do tomorrow. Ila was able to make noise with the wrapper because the teacher had gone out into the hallway to talk to someone. She was glad. Her stomach really needed something. The donuts from this morning had digested and were gone. She laughed. Ila and Paula were in the so called 'Advanced Classes," Sharon was on a regular schedule that is why they had no classes together. Paula and Ila went to their last class and then to chorus. Sharon had to walk home without them. She would wait for Ila on her porch to get the news. When Ila and Paula came out of school Mickey was standing on the corner by the car. He waved them over. Ila looked around to make sure Sharon was not hiding somewhere. Mickey started looking around because Ila was looking around. She made him nervous. They walked over. He said, "get in the car, I will drive you halfway home." They drove in silence. When he got to the fire station, he pulled into the driveway and Ila and Paula got out. Mickey got out of the car and walked over to the girls. "So, the rabbit died," Mickey said. Paula screamed, "This is no time to be funny, what does a rabbit have to do with it." Mickey said, "You are pregnant. I will tell Sugarbear when he gets off work. Paula turned and started walking home. Ila was stuck. What the fuck where they going to do now. Mickey looked at Ila and said, "Meet me in my private space after you have had dinner with the fam." "I can't see you anymore, Sharon might cut her wrist and then what." Ila said. "You are a tornado that has swept us all up and thrown us back into the streets, shit what are we going to do now. We were all best friends until you showed up." Ila turned and walked away. Mickey stood quiet, pulled a cigarette from his pack and lit it. One of the firemen came out of the building. They all knew Mickey, and they greeted each other. The fireman said, "You know that's Jack's daughter, and do you know that motherfucker is crazy." 'Not to worry brother, I am not going to be around much longer, going to the service real soon. By the time he finds out I will be gone. "You better hope so," the fireman said. They stood and talked small talk for a while. They did the bro handshake and Mickey left to go get something to eat, purchase some weed and pick up Sugarbear from work. Ila ran to catch up with Paula. She was crying. Ila stopped her and said, "You could keep the baby, nobody has to know who the father is." "Are you crazy, the only way I am going to get out of this place is to go to college, I don't want to get stuck here with a baby at 14. You will be moving soon, yes, the whole block is talking. I guess your dad had a few at the Café and started running his mouth. You will be gone, and I will be left with a baby by a grown man who will probably leave town. Ila, please help me, tell Mickey to help me." Ila started to cry; she was not sure she could help her friend. She wiped her face with her shirt and forgot she had lipstick on which she was not allowed to wear. She had to stop at Aunt Phyllis' house for the results for Sharon, she would get another top from her, she had three girls, and we were all about the same age. She would not ask Ila any questions, just give her another shirt. She would run upstairs and change when she got home so her mother and grandmother would not see a top that they had never washed before. Ila ran to Aunt Phyllis' house. She told Paula to go home and that they would meet after dinner. "What if there is no dinner at my house," Paula said. "OK, just wait for me on the porch." Ila got to her aunt's house, and she was on the porch. She took one look at Ila's top and said go get a top out of the laundry basket and when you get money, I need .50 cents for the next two weeks to pay for the top you are about to take. Ila walked into the house. Her cousins were not home yet, they were all in high school and had boyfriends and jobs at a local clothing store. Ila grabbed a blouse and left her top in the laundry room. Maybe Aunt Phyllis can get the lipstick off. She put the top on. It was way too big. She stuffed it into her skirt. What a day it had been. She walked out to the porch and her aunt started to laugh. "I don't know how you are going to get away with this outfit, but you are a smart girl, just remember I had nothing to do with your quick change." She started to laugh. "By the way, your friend has a UTI, Urinary Tract Infection. She needs to drink a lot of water, cranberry juice, and soak in the tub with warm water. But really lots of water. You kids don't drink water and it is very important to how the body works." Ila smiled, "Yay all she must do is drink water and cranberry juice and soak in the tub. That is great news." "Oh, and tell her to stop fucking in the woods and you too. If someone else tells me again you are fucking a grown man in the woods, I am going to tell your father, got it," her aunt said sternly. "Do you see how hard it is for me to raise these girls by myself? I got pregnant young and have been struggling ever since, so stop your fast ass before you are living on this street for the rest of your life." Ila was shocked, shit if her father heard that story her ass was going to be split wide open for sure by a belt. Ila nodded her head, kissed her Aunt, walked down the steps in shame and walked home. And there they were the other two shameful girls of Mulford Street sitting on the porch with plates of baked beans and wieners from grandma and red Kool-Aid in plastic cups. Her grandmother saw her coming up the street and got her a plate. Ila's father must not be home because there would be no way they would not be sitting at the table for dinner. As Ila walked up to the house, she took a seat on one of the steps and waited for her grandmother to bring her a plate. When her grandmother came out on the porch she said, your parents are having a grown folk's conversation, so you are eating outside. Your brothers and sister have eaten and are in the backyard. Ila laughed as she ate her beans and wieners. Because a grown folk's conversation meant they were having sex in their bedroom. Paula, Sharon, Grandma, and Ila all started laughing. The beans and wieners were delicious. Ila was so hungry and so was Paula. They both wanted to ask for seconds, but they knew that this meal had to last two days for Ila's family. Ila collected the plates and glasses and took them into the house. She washed the dishes and placed them in the side sink, swept the floor and put a plate on the stove and covered it with foil for her father. She put the rest of the beans and wieners in the refrigerator. Ila came back out to the porch. Her grandmother looked at her and said," Whose top you got on." Ila looked at her grandmother and said, "I spilled soda on my top at school and had to borrow a top from the gym teacher." Grandmother shook her head and said," elephant." That meant she either did not want to hear what you had to say or did not believe what you had to say. Ila laughed. Paula, Sharon, and Ila walked down to the end of the block with all the others hanging out playing four square and double dutch. Paula sat on the steps of Uncle Marvin's house, Sharon and I jumped into the double dutch game. We all had homework, so we only stayed down the street for about 2 hours. It was time to head home. We dropped Paula off first, said our goodbyes. As Ila and Sharon walked home, she told her she had a UTI and she had to drink a lot of water, cranberry juice and take warm baths. If it does not clear up in a week, you have to go back to the health department with one of your parents. Sharon screamed, jumped for joy, and started crying all at the same time. Sharon was fifteen going on sixteen in a couple of weeks she could go to the health department by herself and get birth control. Sharon could not wait for that day. Sharon ran up the steps to her house and was screaming amen, amen. Ila started to laugh. All the fucking and playing around Sharon did and Paula was the one who got pregnant. Ila walked slowly to her house. She was tired and still had homework to do. Everyone was in the house. She went and spoke to everyone and went straight to her room. Her father was asleep. We had to be quiet while he was asleep upstairs. That was not going to be a problem for Ila. She decided to take her bath, clean the bathroom, and then do her homework. When she got out of the tub and cleaned it, brushed her teeth, combed her hair, and placed eight pink curlers in her hair she went off to her room that she shared with her sister to do her homework. But her sister was on the phone talking to her boyfriend. Ila headed for the closet, it was a safe space, and she could think, and the light was bright. The last thing she remembers; her mother was waking her up to get in bed and to say goodnight to my father as he went off to work.

Mickey picked up Sugarbear and gave him the news. Sugarbear was upset. He really liked Paula, but he knew prison time was something he could not do. What if this was the only child he would have in his lifetime. What if it is a boy? All these things were going through his head. Mickey told him that she could not have an abortion without her parents' consent. "Damn Mickey, why did you introduce me to this young girl?" Sugarbear said. Mickey replied, "Brother, you knew how old she was, I told you to play with her not to fuck her, you little head was thinking not your big head and then you kept fucking her without a condom, how dumb are you." Sugarbear just shook his head again. "Man, what the fuck am I going to do," he said. "Well, I have a friend who is a nurse, and she does illegal abortions in her house on Hamilton. You know the one with green and white awnings," Mickey said. "She does them for $150.00 cash, but it is dangerous, you know it is not in a hospital or a clinic it is in her upstairs bedroom that she has changed into a surgery room of sorts." "Got Damn man, that sounds dangerous," Sugarbear said. "So is prison," Mickey said. Sugarbear started to cry. They sat in the car for about an hour. Sugarbear finally spoke. "OK, go talk to your friend, I can have the money by Friday, maybe she can do it on Saturday." Mickey replied," We don't have much time, she won't touch her after her third month, and I think she is already two months. 'OK, he replied, Friday. I will talk to Paula tomorrow when I pick her up for school. "Ok, man, drop me on the corner," Mickey said. "Man, where are you staying these days," Sugarbear asked. "You know you can stay with me." Mickey laughed, "I guess I will be staying with the nurse for the next couple of days to make sure we get that $150.00 price. Sugarbear dropped him at the corner. Sugarbear drove home in pieces. His heart was broken. His seed was going to be destroyed and a young girl's life was going to be turned upside down. He sat in front of his house for some time before going in.

Mickey headed to the nurse's house. He called her from the corner phone booth. She quickly answered the phone, he asked her if she was busy and if she was not busy would she like some company. Of course, she said yes, so Mickey walked to the house in the next block and climbed the 15 steps to get to her front door. He rang the doorbell, and she opened the door in her robe. He was prepared to have sex with her and do whatever to help his friend and Paula. He felt a little guilty if that was an emotion he was capable of. He walked in, grabbed her pussy through her robe and told her to draw him a bath as it had been a long day and she did just that. He would solidify the $150.00 deal tonight and then again in the morning.

Sugarbear did not sleep that night. He called off work first thing the next morning, took a shower and jumped in the car to get Paula for school. She was waiting on the corner as usual. He pulled over to the sidewalk and she jumped in the car. He drove slowly to her school. Then he said, "Go check into homeroom and come back out the side door and let's spend the day together. Paula got to school, ran in and saw Ila and the gang in the hallway. She and Ila went into homeroom, got the roll call and then walked to their next class. Paula told Ila she was ditching and would see her at the end of the day; she and Sugarbear were going to spend the day together. Ila understood. Ila kept walking and Paula took a left down the steps to the side door. Sugarbear was waiting for her. She jumped in the car excited to spend the day with the man that she was in love with. They drove to Squirrel Hill and got fresh bagels and doubled back to Frick Park where they went down under and spent the day on the grass. Coming up from down under they headed to Penn Hills to get an Original Hotdog and fries. After stuffing their faces, they headed to his house. He wanted to just rub her belly and listen to his son's heartbeat as this time next week she would not be pregnant. He talked to her about the lady on Hamilton who would be doing the procedure. He really had no full knowledge but while he could not sleep, he looked through his encyclopedias on illegal abortions.

They enjoyed their day. He drove Paula back to the corner at the time she should be returning from school. He had to go to work the next day and get in some overtime to pay for the abortion.

The week seemed to drag on. Mickey had an appointment for Saturday at noon at the house on Hamilton with the green and white awnings. Sharon's pee pee had not stopped hurting but was not as painful as it was in the beginning of the week. Aunt Phyllis said to give it a week to subside, and it was. Sharon had not seen Mickey but continued to yank on Mr. Burns' dick on the porch and receive what we called an allowance. Ila got up early on Saturday morning and did her chores. Clean the bathroom, clean her bedroom, and wash the kitchen floor. She was done by 11:00 a.m. She did not take a bath, she just washed up and put on a pair of slacks, tennis shoes and a top. She had placed hair rollers in her hair the night before so when she took them out, her hair was filled with curls. She did not comb them out, she just took her fingers and ran it through her hair about five times. The humidity in Pittsburgh did not allow you to have a good hairstyle for longer than three-four hours anyway. She had told her mother that she and Paula were going to a Tom Thumb wedding at Paula's Aunt's church in East Liberty. They were going to take the bus to the Church and then her aunt would bring them home. Paula and Ila were too old to be in the wedding, but Ila told her mother they were helping to get the little kids dressed. Ila's mother Lorraine looked at Ila, like this is some horse shit, but she had to start trusting her. She was becoming a woman very quickly and she could not shelter her forever. Ila's mother told her to be home before the streetlights came on. If the wedding was not over by 5:30 p.m. she would have to leave, especially if she had to take the bus home. Ila agreed and went to her room.

Ila did not sleep well that Friday night but now she was ready. She went to her room and got her backpack and her cosmetics bag. Next, she went into the closet and pulled out five one-dollar bills. Her stash was getting slim. She would have to do more work around the house or go to Aunt Florence's house to help and get paid for it. It was hard being a teenager with no money. She was not old enough to work at a clothing or grocery store, so she had to be skillful on how she earned money. She looked in the mirror that hung on the back of the door. She had to look like she was going to Church. Her grandmother would have something to say about a young lady going to Church in pants. She ran into her brother and sister as she was walking out the door. They had gotten up late and were just doing their chores. Ila's mother had walked to the grocery store with her younger brother and grandma was on the porch. Ila hit the porch and grandma looked at her and said, "I hear you going to Church with Paula," she said. "Yes Grandma, I will be back before it gets dark," Ila replied. Her grandmother shouted out "Elephant." That was her way of saying "Bullshit." Ila did not turn around because somehow, she always knew when Ila was lying. Ila walked fast down the street to Paula's house. She was waiting on the porch at 11:30 a.m. It would take them 20 minutes to walk to the house on Hamilton. Mickey and Sugarbear were going to meet them there. They walked in silence with Paula crying all the way. Ila said, "You don't have to do this, I can be the baby's aunt and you can move with me and my family and nobody would know you had a baby. My mother would not want you to be doing this," Ila said. "Shut up, Ila, I don't want to have a baby and I don't want to live here the rest of my life. I must get out of here, away from my parents, away from Homewood, and start my life again somewhere else after I graduate from high school. I will get a letter written with my mother's signature and take it to the health department and get on birth control, or get Sharon to get them for me, she will be sixteen soon.

No, baby," Paula shouted. With that she stopped crying and started walking faster. She wanted this thing over with. They reached the house and Mickey and Sugarbear were sitting in the car smoking weed. They were both very nervous about this situation. When they saw them coming, they both jumped out of the car. Sugarbear grabbed Paula's hand and started climbing the long staircase. Ila looked at Mickey and he handed her the joint. Ila took the joint and started up the long steps to the porch of the house. Mickey and Sugarbear had already paid nurse Gloria for the procedure. Sugarbear and Paula entered the house and had to climb fifteen more steps to the second floor. The room at the end of the hall was set up like a clinic. Semi hospital bed, flood lamps, instruments on the side of the bed. It smelled like bleach. Nurse Gloria told Paula to take off everything from the waist down. Sugarbear sat in a chair at the far end of the room. Undressed, Paula lay on the bed and the nurse gave her a shot to numb her body from the waist down. Sugarbear got up and held her hand. The nurse talked about the procedure. It would be a D&C abortion which stands for dilation and curettage. I will insert a speculum into her vagina and open it, then take a dilator to enlarge the cervix so that we can have access to the uterus. Then I will insert a suction catheter into the opening and turn on the suction machine. It will be loud because the suction force is 10 to 20 times that of a normal house vacuum cleaner and then the baby is sucked out piece by piece into the machine. To make sure all of the pieces of the baby have been removed I will use a curette to scrape the uterus. She will bleed for about 2-3 days. She should take aspirins or something stronger if available. I will give her pads and aspirin to take with her. Any questions? Sugarbear started to cry and so did Paula. Paula screamed, "I changed my mind, I don't want to do this." Sugarbear said calmly, "We don't have a choice." Sugarbear asked the nurse to continue. In the 80's a woman's voice was still not heard. She gave Paula a mild sedative to calm her during the procedure, her bottom half was already paralyzed. The procedure took about 30 minutes. Sugarbear almost passed out seeing so much blood. He never saw the baby as it was sucked into the machine. Nurse Gloria took all her instruments and placed them into a dishwasher to get them clean. She took rags sprayed with disinfectant and cleaned up the immediate area. She told Sugarbear she would be back in an hour by that time the young lady would be ready to go home. She got up and left the room. Sugarbear could not believe it, she did not even know Paula's name. He started to cry. He pulled himself together and thought it through. There is no way she wanted to know the names or place any kind of value to the person she was giving the abortion to, that would make it too personal, this was a procedure and she treated it as such. Sugarbear sat down and watched Paula like a hawk, if she moved or yelled out, he wanted to be there to hold her hand. And just as the nurse said, Paula started coming around in about an hour. The nurse came in about 10 minutes after Paula started moving around. She asks Paula to get up and to go to the bathroom and to make sure she washed up as there was blood all around her legs and around her vagina. Sugarbear helped her get up and walk to the bathroom. Paula's legs felt very weak. Once in the bathroom, she got very angry and started to cry, then she got happy and started to laugh. She washed up and turned to grab the handle of the door and became dizzy. She stood still for a minute and reached for the handle again and opened the door. Sugarbear had her panties in his hand, and he handed her a pad belt and a pad. The nurse had left a bag filled with sanitary napkins and aspirin. She told Sugarbear he knew the way out. He helped Paula get dressed. Made sure she took four aspirins, and they made their way down the hallway and down all those steps. When they reached the porch, Ila and Mickey stood up. They just continued down the next set of steps to the car. Paula had nothing to say. She did ask Mickey for a joint. He quickly lit one and gave it to her. They rode around for a while. Paula was hungry so they stopped and got burgers and fries and ate in the car. It was getting late, and Paula and Ila had to get home. They left East Liberty and headed back to Homewood. Ila told Sugarbear to drop Paula in front of her house because she should not walk far. It was dinner time, so Ila hoped there were not a hundred people looking to see her get out of Sugarbear's car. Paula got out as straight as she could and walked slowly up the steps to her house. Fortunately, her bedroom was on the first floor, so she just had to go in, go to her room and close the door. When someone came knocking, she could act like she was asleep. Ila decided to stay in the car. She asked Sugarbear to take her to the alley and she would walk home. So, he continued down Mulford Street, making a right and another right and the alleyway was right there. Mickey jumped out with Ila and walked halfway down the alley and returned to his camp. Ila was so glad everyone was in the house having dinner, so she did not have to speak to people. She took the front steps two at a time and ran to the front door. She stopped briefly at the bottom of the steps, spoke to everyone, and ran up the steps to her room. As she landed her last foot on the last step her father came out of the bathroom. "Hi there little girl are you not having dinner," her father said. "No Dad, we had dinner at Church," Ila replied. "Yes, I heard about it, sounds like an elephant," her father said. All Ila could do was laugh and run to her room. She changed her clothes and sat in the window seat. The cool thing about her room is that when you sat in the window seat you could see most of the entire street. They lived in a row house, and they were on the end, and the row house had an alleyway, so it was a great place to have fun. Ila fell asleep in the window seat. She woke up when her father did the house check on his way out the door for work. She woke up again when her father came home from his 11 to 7 shifts. She had a cramp in her neck. You think her sister would have woken her up to get in bed, but she did not. She heard her dad in the hallway and went to greet him on his way to bed. He kissed her on the forehead and said, "Don't go in that bathroom and if you do stay a minute, I want to take a bath and then go to bed." Ila said, "OK" and decided to go to the bathroom in the basement that just had a toilet, but she really had to go. There were mice down there and a coal burning stove that made noise even when it was not on. She walked down the first flight of steps through the dining room, through the kitchen and then down to the basement. It was scary, but she had to go. She turned on the lights and walked slowly so that she could see the mice. For some reason, there were no mice but lots of traps with mice in them. It was her brother's job to clean up the mice. He would be doing that today. She walked gingerly to the toilet and peed a lot. She sat there for a moment and then she heard an ambulance. It sounded like it was coming down Mulford Street. She got up, wiped herself, flushed the toilet and ran up the steps. There was no sink to wash your hands in the basement. She washed her hands in the sink in the kitchen and proceeded to the porch to see what the action was all about. She forgot she did not have on any shoes, but she was just going to the porch. Ila ran out on the porch and her grandmother was already on the porch. "Grandma whose house is the ambulance at," Ila said. "Looks like your friend Paula's house, you know her people are not well," her grandmother said. Ila took off down the street only to see them bringing Paula out on a stretcher and people screaming and horns blowing and sirens going at the same time. Ila would not see Paula again until they were neighbors in Virginia many years later.

Ila's Diamonds IV 2023, Ila's Diamond V 2024